**"Hey, Dad! Look! We don't have all the decorations up,"** Holly cried excitedly from behind the couch, rattling a paper sack.

Something made Leslie glance at Tagg. His gaze was locked on a point a few inches above her head. She looked up and saw the sprig of mistletoe Holly was dangling above her.

"Now you've got to kiss her, Dad," Holly challenged with a giggling laugh.

"That's right, I do," he agreed.

Before Leslie could react, he was leaning toward her. Her pulse skipped a few beats when she found herself gazing into the black centers of his eyes. Her glance lowered to the strong, smooth line of his mouth, coming steadily closer. Her lashes came down a second before she felt the fanning warmth of his breath and the light pressure of his mouth so briefly touching hers. . . .

**Books by Janet Dailey**

# JANET DAILEY

## Mistletoe and Holly

POCKET STAR BOOKS
New York  London  Toronto  Sydney

Originally published by Silhouette Books.

A Pocket Star Book published by
POCKET BOOKS, a division of Simon & Schuster, Inc.
1230 Avenue of the Americas, New York, NY 10020

ISBN: 978-0-671-87508-4

This Pocket Star Books paperback edition December 1985

30  29  28  27  26  25  24  23  22

Map by Ray Lundgren

POCKET STAR BOOKS and colophon are registered trademarks
of Simon & Schuster, Inc.

Front cover illustration by Danilo Ducak

Manufactured in the United States of America

For information regarding special discounts for bulk purchases,
please contact Simon & Schuster Special Sales at
1-800-456-6798 or business@simonandschuster.com.

# Mistletoe and Holly

QUEBEC

N
W   E
S

• Burlington

LAKE CHAMPLAIN

• Montpelier

CONNECTICUT
RIVER

VERMONT

NEW
YORK

NEW HAMPSHIRE

VERMONT

MASSACHUSETTS

# CHAPTER

# 1

THE SUNLIGHT GLISTENED on the snow's icy crust, creating a diamond shimmer that dazzled Leslie's eyes. A frown of irritation crossed her usually smooth features as she made a one-handed search of her purse on the car seat beside her, looking for her sunglasses without taking her attention from the road. The snowplows had cleared the road two or three days before, judging by the melting piles of mud-spattered snow along the shoulders, but there were still slick patches where the plow blade hadn't scraped all the way to the road's surface.

Skidding on one of those icy patches was definitely not on her list of thrills she wanted to experience. Leslie Stiles had already had her fill of accidents for one winter. Her hand's blind search came up with the sunglasses which she immediately slipped onto the bridge of her nose, her hazel eyes instantly feeling the relief from the sun's glare on the sparkling white mantle of snow that covered the Vermont countryside.

A stop sign stood at the crossroads and Leslie slowed the car to a halt as she approached it. Melting snow dripped onto the car roof from an overhanging tree branch. The drops made a tinny sound as they landed. A dirty pickup truck that might have been green had the right of way. Her fingers tapped the steering wheel impatiently as she waited for its putting speed to carry it across the intersection.

The strain of the drive from Manhattan was beginning to show on her—the strain and her own physical pain. Leslie attempted to shift into a more comfortable position, but the thick plaster cast on her left leg severely limited movement and position. It was a lucky thing the car had a lot of leg room—and an automatic transmission. There was a steady throb of pain that tensed all her nerves and planted her teeth together. In her purse, Leslie had a bottle of pain pills, prescribed by the doctor, but they made her sleepy so she hadn't taken any, certain she could grit her way through the trip to her aunt's home. It was turning into more of an ordeal than she had thought it would be.

The pickup passed and Leslie made her turn onto the intersecting highway. She clung to the knowledge that she only had a few more miles to go. Already she could see the white spire of the church steeple poking above the tops of the trees.

There was a distinct New England character to the village nestled in the mountain fastness. There was something changeless and nostalgic about its steepled church and village green, and its old houses all in neat repair. Too many artists had captured towns like it on canvas, which gave even strangers the sense of coming home.

Leslie wasn't a stranger, but neither did she view it as home. When she approached her aunt's two story Victorian-style house on the outskirts of the rural community, she saw it merely as a refuge, a place to recuperate from this damnable broken leg, and avoid all of December's holiday hoopla.

No attempt had been made to clear the driveway of snow, although there was a set of parallel tracks going in and out. Leslie slowed her car to make the turn, barely noticing the man pulling a red-suited child on a sled in the next yard. The car tires crunched in the crusty snow as she wheeled the vehicle into the drive, stopping short of the side door.

Relief sighed through her strained nerves as she removed the sunglasses and smoothed a side of her sand-colored hair where it was pulled sleekly back and secured at the nape of her neck to trail between her shoulder blades. As December went, it was a mild day with the temperature hovering above the freezing mark, so Leslie didn't bother to put on the rusty-brown, fake fur jacket that lay on the passenger seat. It would only hamper her movements, and maneuvering her cast-rigid leg out of the car wasn't going to be an easy task.

Her crutches were propped against the passenger door. She pulled them over, so they'd be within reach once she was outside, then opened her door. Scooting sideways, she managed to gain enough room to swing her left leg around and aim it out the door.

The sound of footsteps and sled runners cutting through the snow's crust signaled the approach of the next door neighbor as she edged forward to test the footing before she made a one-legged attempt to stand up. It was something she hadn't mastered too well as yet, so she regarded his appearance at that moment as ill-timed. Broken legs and graceful movements simply did not go together.

Her smile was a bit tight when he hove into view with the sled in tow. Leslie tried to keep the flash of annoyance out of her eyes as she glanced toward him. He was tall, easily six foot if not more, which forced her to tip her head back in order to focus her gaze higher. A network of smile lines fanned out from the corners of his icy blue eyes, framed by dark, male lashes. The winter sun had added the finishing touches to the tan the summer sun had started, giving a certain ruggedness to his leanly handsome features. Hatless, his dark hair had a black sheen to it, thick and attractively rumpled by a playful breeze.

If it hadn't been for the strain of the drive and the nagging pain in her leg, Leslie probably would have found him physically disturbing. But her least concern at the moment was how good-looking he was. She just wanted to get into her aunt's house, take a pain pill, and lie down.

His gaze glittered down on her with friendly interest, yet managed to take her apart at the same time. He observed the annoyance behind the polite smile she gave him, the high cheekbones that kept her features from being average, and the rounded right knee where her long skirt had ridden up higher than her fur-lined winter boot. A stretched-out woolen sock protected the bare toes that peeked out of her left leg cast.

"Let me give you a hand," he offered and reached out to give her the steadying support of his grip while she held onto the door with her other hand.

"Thank you," Leslie murmured when she was upright and precariously balanced on one foot.

"You must be Leslie," he guessed and kept a light hold on her arm until she was more sure of her footing. "Your aunt said you'd be arriving today. I'm Tagg Williams and this is my daughter, Holly. We live in the house next door."

"How do you do." It was a polite phrase with little meaning behind it. Leslie wasn't intentionally trying to be rude or unfriendly. She was just tired and plagued by the dull pain of her injury.

The little girl had climbed off the sled and waded through the hard snow for a closer look at the white cast on Leslie's leg. She was all of six years old. Her beguilingly innocent face was framed by the red hood of her parka trimmed in white fur. She was wearing a pair of matching red snow pants and white boots, and a pair of white, furry mittens. Her eyes were a darker blue than her father's and blessed with long, naturally curling dark lashes.

"Holly, get the crutches for her, will you?" Tagg Williams took it upon himself to make the request of his daughter, so Leslie wouldn't have to make the hopping turn to reach them.

"Sure." The young girl half-climbed into the seat to drag the metal crutches out by their padded tops and gave them to Leslie.

"Thank you." She managed to keep her balance

long enough to maneuver the crutches, one under each arm, and let them take her weight.

"Did you have an accident skiing?" the little girl asked.

Her mouth slanted wryly. "Nothing so glamourous, I'm afraid," Leslie replied. "There was a patch of ice on the sidewalk in front of my apartment building. I slipped and fell and broke my leg."

"I bet it hurt." She gave Leslie a wide-eyed look of sympathy.

"It did. It hurt a lot." Leslie didn't believe in downplaying the harsh facts of reality, especially with children. In the long run, honesty would do them more good than pretence or white lies.

Hinges creaked when the storm door to the house was pushed open. A fairly tall, gray-haired woman stood in the opening, dressed in a pair of loose-fitting brown slacks, a heavily knitted tan pullover with an orange and brown blouse underneath.

"She's here, Mrs. Evans!" The little girl named Holly hurried toward the side door to announce the arrival to Leslie's aunt. "I saw her car drive in!"

"And you guessed right away that she was my niece. That's very clever of you, Holly." As a former schoolteacher, it was an ingrained habit for Patsy Evans to comment on a child's observation, which

7

she did warmly, but not effusively. Then she greeted her niece. "Did you have a good trip up, Leslie?"

"Yes. Thankfully there was very little traffic." The rutted tracks in the snow made by previous vehicles made it difficult to negotiate with the crutches when Leslie tried to keep her balance and open the rear car door where her bags were.

"I'll bring your luggage in." Tagg Williams moved effortlessly to intercept her and eliminate the need for the attempt.

"Thank you." This time her smile was much more genuine in its show of gratitude. His alert gaze seemed to notice that, too, and lingered on the curving movement of her lips. But Leslie was already busy making the turn toward the house, so she wasn't aware of his heightened interest.

"Most of the traffic comes during the weekend when the skiers descend on the area," her aunt replied to Leslie's initial remark and watched with sharp concern while Leslie awkwardly approached the house.

The concrete steps leading to the back door were clear of any snow or ice, although they were wet. Icicles dripped water from the eaves overhead, plopping and splattering when the large droplets hit the ground. Leslie paused in front of the bottom step.

"Can you manage all right?" her aunt asked, ready to go to her aid if she couldn't.

"Three steps I can manage," Leslie replied with a short, dry laugh. "It's the three flights of stairs to my apartment that were impossible." Then she remembered. "Damn. I left my purse in the car."

"Holly will get it for you." Autocratically Patsy Evans motioned to the young girl to fetch Leslie's purse.

"It's in the front seat." She called the information to the blue-eyed girl in the red snowsuit who was already dashing toward the car.

With her aunt holding the door open, Leslie mounted the steps one at a time and swung across the threshold to enter the house. It had been five years since she had last visited her aunt, yet time hadn't seemed to change anything.

The large kitchen with its birch cabinets looked just the same. The pussycat clock on the wall was still swinging its pendulum tail, marking off the seconds. Even the plaid curtains at the windows were the same pattern if not the same curtains that had hung there before. It was funny that she remembered these little details after all this time. It wasn't as if she'd grown up in the house, or even been a frequent visitor to her aunt's home.

Actually, it had only been during her college

years that Leslie had become really acquainted with her aunt. It was a case of liking the person, rather than a relative. Patsy Evans had a keen sense of humor and a ready smile, but Leslie was drawn more by her aunt's no-nonsense attitude. Patsy was her father's sister, and it was difficult to imagine two people with more divergent personalities.

As her scanning gaze finished its sweep of the kitchen and stopped on her aunt, Leslie smiled. There was contentment in her otherwise tired expression.

"I always did like this house," she declared. "It's so strong and solid."

"Yes." There was a musing quality about her aunt's agreement. "It's what you look for in a home, isn't it? Yet those same traits are regarded as unflattering in a person."

The rattle of the doorknob interrupted any reply Leslie might have made. Then a small hand succeeded in turning it and little Holly Williams came into the house, followed by her father with Leslie's suitcases under his arms. Both stopped on the large rug so they wouldn't track on the floor.

"Here's your purse." Holly stretched to hand it to her, careful not to overbalance and step off the rug with the snow-wet boots.

"Thank you, Holly." Leslie rested her weight on

the crutches and leaned to take it from the girl. "And thank you, Mr. Williams, for bringing my luggage in." It seemed she had been thanking the pair ever since she had arrived.

"You had your hands full. It was the least I could do." The corners of his mouth deepened in a smile as he glanced pointedly at her crutches. Then his attention was swinging to her aunt. "Where would you like me to set them, Mrs. Evans?"

"There by the counter, is fine," she nodded and turned to Leslie. "I don't believe you've met my new neighbors, have you Leslie?"

"We more or less introduced ourselves outside," Tagg Williams inserted, flashing another smile at her.

"Good," her aunt stated in her typically decisive voice. "I was just going to put some water on to heat for tea. Would you like to stay and have a cup with us, Taggart?"

"Another time, perhaps," he refused as his astute blue eyes skimmed Leslie with another thorough glance. "Your niece looks tired after her journey." With one hand, he was reaching behind him to open the door and steering his daughter in that direction with the other. "Enjoy your stay." The last was directed to Leslie.

Something in his final look touched her feminine core that had been too tired to care about anything before, and attracted her interest. She managed to assimilate a few impressions like the width of his shoulders under the heavy winter jacket and the lean-jawed strength of his profile, then the inner door was closing behind him, followed by the storm door.

The corners of her mouth were pulled down by a dry smile as she glanced sideways at her aunt, busy at the sink filling the teakettle with water. "Why is it the good-looking ones are always married?"

Patsy Evans laughed, a low sound that came from her throat. "I'm not so sure he is."

"Oh?" Leslie opened her purse and took out the prescription bottle, then hobbled on her crutches to the sink for a glass of water.

"Unless he has locked his wife in the attic, I haven't seen a sign of anyone except Taggart and the little girl since they moved in the first of November." She set the teakettle on the stove's gas burner and lighted the flame with a match. "I really can't tell you whether he's divorced or widowed. Since he has never volunteered the information, I have respected his privacy and not asked."

"His daughter certainly seemed happy and well-behaved for the offspring of a single parent." Leslie made the observation almost absently as she took the prescribed dosage of medicine and washed the pills down with water. Being the only child of divorced parents herself, Leslie had firsthand knowledge of what that was like. "How old is she?"

"Holly is six years old now but she'll be seven the day after Christmas. She was obviously named for the season." Patsy Evans didn't pause from her task to answer the question as she took a set of cups and saucers from the cupboard and placed them on the counter.

"What does he do?" Leslie wondered, again aloud.

"You mean for a living?" Her aunt stopped to think. "I don't believe he's said. He doesn't talk about himself very much. For all his outward friendliness and charm, he seems to be a private person." She slid a glance at Leslie, curiosity gleaming in her shrewd, brown eyes. "Are you in the market for a husband with a ready-made family, Leslie?" she chided, and let the affection in her voice take any sting from her words.

"Hardly." Leslie pushed away from the sink and gripped her crutches. "I've seen enough bad marriages to keep me single for the rest of my life." Not just her parents, but those of her friends as well.

"You'll change your mind someday," her aunt declared with certainty.

Leslie glanced at her, then laughed. "You're probably right. What is it they say about 'famous last

13

words?' " It was a rhetorical question that trailed off tiredly at the end.

Patsy Evans took a closer look at her niece and suggested, "Why don't you go into the living room and get that leg propped up? I'll bring the tea when it's ready."

The prospect was too inviting for Leslie to refuse. "I think I'll do that and give this pain pill a chance to work." As she pivoted on her good leg and swung the crutches around to start for the living room, one of the crutches banged into a kitchen chair. "I'm like a bull in a china shop with these things," she grumbled in irritation. "I'd like to know why it's more difficult to maneuver on four legs than it is on two."

"Coordination will come with practice," her aunt assured.

"I'll be a pro with these things by the time this cast comes off in five weeks," Leslie agreed and clumped out of the kitchen.

Like the house itself, the furniture in it was strong and solidly built, some of the pieces bordering on antique. The thick cushions on the gold corduroy sofa were firm, indicating to Leslie that the upholstery was new, but the sofa wasn't. She sat at one end and lifted her casted leg onto the cushions, plumping handmade crewelwork pillows behind her back for additional support. Closing her eyes, she let the quiet of the old house spill over her. Peace was something she had always appreciated, and it was no less precious to her now at twenty-five.

A reflective expression stole over her features in repose. It was true that, despite all her antimarriage remarks, she secretly desired a lifelong partner to love, and to be loved by him. There had been moments in her life when she had thought she had found him, only to discover fundamental differences of opinion. Those relationships, like most others, had died an early death. Leslie knew she was wary; sometimes she wondered if she wasn't expecting too much, but she wasn't prepared to settle for less.

A sigh broke from her lips. An instant later, she heard her aunt's footsteps entering the living room. She opened her eyes, smelling the fragrance of freshly brewed tea. A cup was set on the table within easy reach for Leslie as her aunt took a seat in the matching armchair that faced the fireplace.

"How's your father? I haven't heard from him lately." Her aunt asked to be filled in on the family.

"He and Millie and the kids are spending the holidays at their condominium in Hawaii. They're all fine." Both of her parents had remarried after their divorce when Leslie was fourteen. Each had stepchildren.

Having wanted brothers and sisters all through

childhood, she had been disillusioned when she had finally acquired both. The sibling rivalry and setting parent against stepparent were painful things for her; almost as painful as the way her parents had tore at her, trying to be the sole object of her love and depriving the other of her affection. Her parents' marriage and divorce had both been fought with Leslie as the battleground. Growing up had been unpleasant, dimming what few happy memories she possessed.

"Hawaii," her aunt repeated. "It must be wonderful to escape all this snow and cold."

"As soon as Daddy was notified about my fall, he had prepaid tickets waiting at the airport for me to fly over there and stay with them." Her grimace showed her opinion of that invitation. "You know what it's like at Christmas—everyone trying to outdo the other and complaining if their present isn't as expensive as the one they gave. The endless parties. Decorations all over the place." She shook her head to show her dislike for such things. "Needless to say, Daddy was upset when I told him I wasn't coming." There was no humor in her laugh. "He was convinced I was going to Mother's for the holidays. She drove into New York from Baltimore just to take me home with her. Then she got angry because she thought I was going to Hawaii."

"Why didn't you tell them you were coming here?" A dark gray eyebrow was lifted in puzzled amusement.

"I did, but they didn't believe me." Leslie shrugged. "They thought I was just saying that to avoid hurting their feelings."

"Your mother and father are too much alike. Both of them are too intense, too quick to anger, and too possessive," she pronounced with a degree of sadness. "A marriage of opposites is better than that. One has a stabilizing influence on the other."

"Do you really think so?" Leslie was skeptical.

"You need to have the basis of love and common interests, but with two different personalities involved," her aunt elaborated on her initial statement.

"I suppose that makes sense, as long as one didn't try to change the other," she conceded. "Either way, I'm glad I'm here. And I'm really grateful that you're letting me stay with you."

"It's a big, old house. There is always plenty of room for you to come anytime you want," her aunt insisted. "Besides, I had no plans for the Christmas holidays, except to spend it quietly here. I suppose we could get a tree if you want."

"No. I don't believe in that nonsense," Leslie stated firmly. "I've been called a female Scrooge, but I think Christmas has lost its meaning. It's all decorations and gifts and parties. It's an excuse to celebrate rather than a reason."

"That's a cynical attitude." The remark was almost an admonition.

"It's true," she insisted. "It used to be Christmas merchandise was never displayed in stores until after Thanksgiving. Now it's on the shelves before Halloween. Personally, I think they should ban Christmas."

"Unfortunately the economy would suffer if that was attempted," Patsy Evans murmured dryly and changed the subject. "How's your job? It was certainly understanding of your employer to grant you a leave of absence until after New Year's."

"Mr. Chambers had planned to be gone most of the month attending a sales conference anyway, and he always takes off a few days before Christmas, so there wouldn't have been much for me to do at the office except handle the mail and answer the phone. The receptionist can do that." She knew her boss too well to believe he had been motivated solely by compassion. He had given her a leave of absence because it was both practical and economical.

"Then both of you are benefiting from it since you don't have to worry about going back and forth to work in bad weather. You'll have a chance to rest while your leg heals," her aunt reasoned.

"Yes." It just seemed bad luck that she had broken her leg at this time of year, presuming there was a good time for an accident like that. She had an aversion to the holiday season, a holdover from her childhood probably. Usually she could escape it with work or physical activity. Both those were taken from her.

She sipped at her tea and tried not to think about it.

# CHAPTER

## 2

CHRISTMAS SEEMED INESCAPABLE. Nearly every other song the disc jockey played on the radio was oriented toward the season. After trying for almost an hour to tune in other stations, Leslie gave up and switched the radio off. She had already read two books since she had arrived at her aunt's. She liked reading, but not all the time.

In desperation, she picked up a deck of cards and propped her leg on a kitchen chair to begin playing solitaire to pass the time until her aunt returned from her shopping trip. Leslie wished now she hadn't decided to stay at the house.

The knock at the side door startled her. No car had driven in; there hadn't been the sound of footsteps climbing the back steps to the door; and no movement in the kitchen window facing the driveway. Leslie pushed the cards into a pile at the end of the table and grabbed for her crutches. With growing deftness, she maneuvered them under her arms and swung toward the door in long strides. Steam and frost covered the glass pane in the door, preventing Leslie from seeing who was outside.

In New York, she wouldn't have dreamed of opening the door without knowing who was out there, but this was Vermont. She opened the inner door and saw a short, red-coated child standing on the other side of the storm door. Leslie pushed it open too, her glance running past the little girl, but there was no sign of her father.

"Hello." The hood to her red snow jacket wasn't covering her head, revealing long, shining black hair. Its blackness made the girl's eyes seem all the more blue.

"Hello, Holly." Leslie was a bit confused as she glanced at the paper sack the girl clutched against the front of her unbuttoned jacket. A pair of blue barrettes secured the black hair swept away from her temples.

"May I come in?" she asked with a look that fairly beamed with friendly warmth.

"Of course." She shifted her crutches to back out of the opening and let the young girl step inside.

Holly paused on the rug and painstakingly wiped all traces of snow and moisture from her shoes. "I forgot to wear my boots." There was a hint of mischief in the rueful expression. "My dad's probably gonna be mad when he finds out." But she obviously wasn't concerned.

"Was there something you wanted?" Leslie still wasn't too sure about the reason for this visit. Her aunt hadn't indicated the little girl was in the practice of coming over.

"I saw Mrs. Evans drive away a while ago and I thought you might like some company," she declared and walked to the kitchen table to lay her paper sack on it.

"That's very thoughtful of you." Leslie had been wishing for someone to talk to, but she wryly wondered if her desperation for company stretched to conversing with a six-going-on-seven-year-old girl.

"I know," the girl agreed blandly and shrugged out of her jacket, draping it on a chair back. Underneath the jacket, she was wearing a pair of blue corduroy overalls and a white blouse with a ruffled collar. She managed to look both the little lady and the tomboy. "Is it all right if I call you

22

Leslie? Dad said I should ask before I called you that," she explained to Leslie over her shoulder.

"I don't mind if you call me Leslie." A little bemused, she edged around the girl to resume her seat in the kitchen chair.

"Do you want me to put your crutches somewhere?" Holly volunteered.

"No, that's all right," Leslie refused gently. "I'll just stand them up against the wall where I can reach them."

"I always thought Leslie was a boy's name, but Daddy said it can be a girl's name, too." She emptied the contents of her paper sack onto the table. There were a dozen pieces of red and green construction paper, a bottle of glue, and a pair of blunt-ended, child's scissors.

"I guess it must be true since my name is Leslie and I'm a girl," she offered, containing an amused smile. "What's all this you have here?"

"I remembered when I was sick with the measles, it made me feel better if I had something to do. So I brought this over. I thought you might like to help me make a paper-chain to hang on our Christmas tree."

"I see." Actually what Leslie saw was the irony of the situation. She, who abhorred the commercialized Christmas and all its trappings, was being asked by a little girl to help make a Christmas decoration.

She liked children, so how could she refuse without appearing heartless and cold.

"I can show you if you don't know how to make them. It's real easy," Holly assured her and picked up the scissors to cut a strip of green construction paper crosswise. "You start with a piece of paper like this— it can be red or green—then you glue the ends together like this." She squirted a glob of white glue on one end and stuck them together with the excess glue oozing out the sides. "Then you take a different color." She picked up the red paper and crookedly cut off another strip. "And you put it through the first one before you glue it. That's how you make a chain."

"That's very good." Leslie managed to force an approving nod.

Holly wrinkled her nose in rueful disagreement. "But I don't cut straight."

"It just takes practice."

"Why don't you cut the paper and I'll paste it together? It will go faster," the girl suggested with bright-eyed eagerness.

Leslie opened her mouth twice, but couldn't find an adequate excuse to refuse. "All right."

She took the small scissors Holly held out to her. The handles were so small she could barely get her fingers in them, but she began cutting. The edges were so dull it was closer to sawing. Holly pulled a kitchen chair closer to Leslie and sat on her knees to begin the task of pasting the chain together.

"Do you have a boyfriend, Leslie?" she asked.

Leslie threw her a look, wondering what prompted that question. "No."

"I do. His name is Bobby Jenkins and he always sits beside me at Sunday School. He says he wants to marry me." She frowned and tipped her head to one side to look at Leslie. "Has anyone ever wanted to marry you?"

"Yes, a couple of boys have asked me," she admitted and tried not to appear too amused by the subject matter. Neither did she explain the last serious marriage proposal had been when she was a freshman in college.

"How come you didn't marry them?"

"Because I didn't love them." Leslie kept cutting the strips of colored construction paper, pausing now and then to flex her fingers.

Holly sighed heavily and began pasting again. "I'm too young to be in love."

"You are a bit young." Leslie had trouble keeping her tongue out of her cheek.

"Do you think my daddy is handsome?" Holly wanted to know. "A lot of women do."

"Yes, he's a good-looking man." She tried to

sound disinterested, and failed, although she doubted that his daughter knew the difference.

"Are you going to fall in love with my daddy like they do?"

That was going too far. "Holly—" Leslie rested both hands on the tabletop and gave the child a look that was a mixture of exasperation and amusement, "—I only met your father once. I don't even know him. I've hardly even talked to him."

She thought about that for a minute. "After you get to know him, then are you going to fall in love with him?"

Leslie didn't make another attempt to answer the question. "Where do you get ideas like this?"

"They just come to me," Holly declared with a shrug and an innocently batting blink of her eyes. Bending over the table, she squirted glue from the bottle onto a band of red paper.

"It might work better if you used less paste," Leslie suggested as it went on the table. At least it was the kind that washed off with soap and water.

"Okay." There were already a dozen links to the paper chain. Holly stretched it out to see how it looked. "It's really going to be pretty on our tree, isn't it?"

"Um-hmm." It was an agreeing sound, which allowed Leslie to stop short of voicing an outright approval for the tree-trimming tradition that had lost its meaning over the years.

The double barrier of the storm windows muffled the voice calling outside the house. "Holly!"

"Whoops! That's my daddy." She scrambled off her perch on the chair and darted to the door.

"Your coat—" Leslie protested, thinking the little girl intended to run outside without it.

But she only opened the two doors and stuck her head outside. "I'm over here, Daddy!" Without waiting for a reply, Holly blithely shut the doors and skipped back to her chair.

Leslie stared, slightly taken aback by the child's lack of concern. While Holly seemed a little precocious, she hadn't acted spoiled or overindulged. If it wasn't the latter, she was certainly extremely confident of herself.

From the corner of her eye, Leslie caught the movement of someone passing the kitchen window. That was followed by a knock at the door. She didn't need three guesses as to who it might be.

"Come in." She called out the permission to enter, rather than hobble ungracefully to the door to admit Tagg Williams. Unconsciously she bit her lips to force color into them, aware she hadn't bothered to put on makeup.

The storm door opened, then the inner door, and

her aunt's tall, dark neighbor walked in. His strong and sun-browned features were wearing a curious expression, his piercing blue eyes slightly narrowed. Without the dullness of fatigue and soreness, Leslie absorbed the full impact of him beyond the striking coloration of coal black hair and light blue eyes. Lines were grooved into his lean cheeks, indicating the frequency of his smiles. His mouth was thin and firm, clearly defined. There was a vitality about him, a virility that came from the combination of the whole rather than any single part of him. Leslie thought she glimpsed a sense of humor perpetually lurking in the blue of his eyes.

"So this is where you got off to." He eyed his daughter with a trace of reproval.

"I'm sorry. I thought you knew she was here." Leslie had presumed Holly had told him she was coming over. Even though it wasn't her fault, she felt a little guilty for not questioning the girl.

"I thought she was playing in the kitchen until I became suspicious over how quiet she was." His mouth lifted in a faint smile. "I guess parents develop a sixth sense about such things."

"I was going to tell you, Daddy, but you were busy," Holly explained in defense of her oversight. "I knew you wouldn't mind. And I knew I'd hear you call."

"You still should have asked." He walked to

Holly's chair and lightly tugged at a strand of black hair, then rested his hands on her shoulders.

"I knew Leslie was here alone. I thought we could keep each other company. Look." She held up the paper chain. "See what we've been making for the tree."

"Let me guess—you did the pasting and made the chains while Leslie got the boring job of cutting the paper," Tagg Williams said dryly.

"She cuts straighter than me," Holly defended the system she'd arranged.

"I didn't mind," Leslie inserted. Actually, his little girl had livened up a dull afternoon for her.

"Thanks." When he looked at her, she felt warmed by his smile. If she wasn't convinced she had passed the blushing stage, she might have believed she had. But it was just an inner glow that heated her skin. Then he was patting his daughter's shoulder. "Get your things gathered up so we can go home. You've taken enough of Leslie's time."

"We haven't finished the chain." Holly looked at the paper still to be cut.

"You and I will finish it tonight. How's that?" He slanted her a grin with a downward tilt of his head.

"Okay." She began scooping her papers, scissors, and glue into the sack, leaving the incomplete paper chain to add last. "We're going out into the woods on Friday to cut our own Christmas tree. Why don't you come with us, Leslie?" she invited without checking with her father.

"Thank you, but—" She paused in time to check the impulse to inform Holly that she thought it was a crime to cut down a valuable tree just to hang some ornaments on it.

"—I don't think Leslie would have much fun hiking through the snow on crutches, Holly," Tagg inserted an excuse in the pause.

"She could ride on my sled and you could pull her," Holly suggested, finding a quick solution to the problem.

"Thanks, but as clumsy as I am, I'd probably fall off," Leslie refused.

Holly appeared to reluctantly accept her decision not to accompany them on their tree-cutting expedition. That idea was no sooner abandoned than another occurred to her. "Would you like us to cut you and Mrs. Evans a tree?" she asked, then turned to her father to verify it. "We could do that, couldn't we?"

"We could." He nodded.

"My aunt and I have talked it over and we aren't going to have a tree this year," Leslie stated to eliminate the offer.

"But you've got to have a tree!" Holly looked

properly shocked. "Santa won't have any place to put your presents if you don't have a tree."

In her opinion, the myth of Santa Claus was a cruel hoax perpetuated by unthinking adults. She remembered her own traumatic discovery that he didn't exist when she was Holly's age. She had cried for two days.

Leslie worked to control her expression so her personal opinion of the subject wouldn't show. After all, it wasn't her place to correct the child's mistaken belief in something that didn't exist, but she really felt her father should. Some of that inner conviction must have shown in her eyes, because when she glanced at Tagg Williams, the measuring study of his gaze took on a mocking gleam.

She bristled ever so slightly before finally replying to Holly's remark. "My aunt and I have decided we don't want a tree," she stated again. "So I guess Santa Claus will just have to pass this house without leaving any gifts."

The large pair of china blue eyes viewed Leslie with solemn roundness. "Santa wouldn't do that unless you've been bad." She seemed worried that Leslie might have been bad.

"I don't believe Leslie has been a bad girl." Amusement was edging his mouth as Tagg affectionately squeezed his daughter's arm in reassurance. There was no mistaking the mocking light that danced so disturbingly in his eyes when he glanced at Leslie. "I think Leslie is saying that she doesn't believe in Santa Claus."

Holly's mouth opened in a round circle of discovery. Then a pitying expression stole over her innocently drawn features. "Don't you believe in Santa Claus, Leslie?"

"No." There was absolutely no reason to lie about it. Still, she felt defensive about admitting it to a child. She was irritated with Holly's father for putting her on the spot, so she challenged him. "Do you believe in Santa Claus?"

"Of course," he answered without hesitation as a smile broke across his face.

"Gee, I'm sorry you don't believe in Santa Claus anymore," Holly declared sadly. "Maybe Daddy and me can help you believe in him again."

She had the uncanny sensation she was being backed into a corner, assaulted from two sides. Leslie was determined to stand her ground and not be talked into an admission that was contrary to her beliefs. "I don't think you can, Holly." Her voice was cool and firm. It seemed wisest to bring this discussion to a close. "I enjoyed your company today. Maybe you can come visit me again. Only the next time, be sure and tell your father where you're going."

"I will." Holly's response seemed more offhand than assuring. Picking up her snow jacket, she thrust a hand through an armhole. Tagg helped her find the second. "Since Leslie doesn't want to come with us when we get the tree, maybe she can come over to our house and help us decorate it. She did help me make the chain."

"We'll see." His glance at Leslie seemed to say that he knew she would refuse if the question was put to her now. She suspected he wanted to avoid letting his daughter suffer any more rejections of her invitations. Holly gathered up her paper sack and jumped off the chair to walk to the door. "Where are your boots?"

Holly peered up at him through her long lashes, so innocent and so beguiling. "I forgot to wear them," she admitted. "But I wiped my feet real good so I wouldn't track on Mrs. Evans' floor."

He didn't appear completely mollified by her reply. "Next time—" he began on a warning note.

"—I won't forget to wear them. I promise," Holly inserted quickly and turned the doorknob. As she pulled it open, she looked across her shoulder at Leslie, smiling and waving. "Bye, Leslie!"

"Bye," Leslie responded, but Holly was already pushing open the storm door.

Tagg paused by the door, his hand holding it

open. A fine thread of tension seemed to run through the room, tying them together. Her heartbeat seemed louder, but it might have been just the sudden silence. She was fascinated by the polar blue color of his eyes, but their look was anything but cold. There was a latent sexuality about him that Leslie hadn't noticed before. It was no wonder that his daughter had observed that women fell in love with him. It would be so easy. Mentally she pulled back from the thought. It seemed to break the spell that had held them both silent.

"I hope Holly wasn't too much trouble," he said.

"She wasn't." The words, the subject matter seemed all wrong. It was an empty communication, a poor substitute for another that neither of them were prepared to make.

"She'll probably be back over another time to visit," Tagg inserted, almost as an amused warning. "If you're busy, just send her on home."

"Okay."

"Take care of that leg." It was said in parting, along with a quick, disturbing smile. Then the two doors were shutting behind him. Leslie had a glimpse of him through the window as he made a skimming descent of the back steps and cut across the driveway to catch up with his daughter.

The house seemed quieter and emptier. Leslie reached for the deck of cards and idly began shuffling them to play another game of solitaire.

After lunch on Friday, Leslie volunteered to do the dishes. When the last pan was rinsed and stacked in the dishdrainer to dry, she pulled the sink stopper and washed the suds down the drain. Hopping on one leg and using the crutches for balance, she tugged the terry towel from its wall rack and wiped the moisture from her hands. Her aunt was bending down to search through one of the bottom cupboards.

"What are you doing?" Leslie asked with a half-smile as her aunt nearly crawled inside the cupboard in her search.

"I'm trying to find my roaster pan." Her voice came hollowly from the inside of the cupboard. "I thought I'd fix a pork roast for dinner tonight. Ahh, here it is."

There was a noisy rattle of pans before she backed out of the cupboard with a mottled gray roaster pan and lid in hand. Patsy Evans pushed to her feet and set the pan on the countertop.

"At the rate I've been eating since I came here, I'll need to go on a diet before I leave." Usually

Leslie was too busy at work to eat three full meals a day.

"We'll diet together when the time comes," her aunt declared with a twinkling look. "It's such a pleasure to cook for two people and not be faced with a refrigerator full of leftovers."

"There aren't many recipes to fix a dish for just one person," Leslie agreed. "Is there anything I can do to help?"

She barely got the question out when someone knocked at the side door. "Yes." Her aunt changed the negative response she had been about to make. "You can answer that."

After being on crutches for two weeks, Leslie was becoming adept at ambulating with them. She moved with relative swiftness to the door, balanced her weight on one crutch, and opened the door with her free hand. She was startled and a little unnerved to find Tagg Williams standing at the threshold, holding the storm door open with his shoulder.

"Hi." His glittering gaze made its usual run down her length before coming back to hold her glance.

"Hello." Leslie was instantly conscious of the baggy pair of gray slacks she had borrowed from her aunt. None of hers would fit over the plaster cast.

They were hardly flattering to her slim figure. The same was true of the sloppy-fitting maroon sweater. It almost made her look flat-chested.

"Taggart, come in." Her aunt had glanced across the room to identify her visitor. She didn't believe in shortening a person's given name, and never abbreviated his. "—Before you let all the cold air in," she added the admonishment.

Leslie shifted to one side so he had room to step in and close the door. He didn't bother to unbutton the charcoal gray wool parka he was wearing, which indicated he didn't intend to stay long. Leslie had always considered herself to be tall, at five foot six inches in her stockinged feet, but standing beside him, she was conscious of his superior height. The top of her head would just brush his chin, if she were closer. The latter thought sent a small quiver over her spine.

"I came by to see if Leslie wouldn't change her mind and come along with us on our search for a Christmas tree." Tagg stated the reason for his visit, not letting his gaze stray from her face. "I borrowed an old dogsled for you to ride in so you won't have to worry about falling off Holly's sled. I even have a couple of old fur blanket robes. They might smell a little musty but they'll keep you warm."

Leslie was slightly stunned at the trouble he'd

taken to insure she'd be comfortable, but none of that altered one salient point. "I don't think you understand. I don't believe in chopping down trees just to use them for Christmas decorations."

"Are you an ecology nut?" he countered smoothly, a suggestion of a smile showing around the corners of his mouth. He gave no sign that he was deterred by her response.

"No. Not exactly." Leslie faltered at the unexpected question. She supported many of the ecology issues, but she wasn't an extremist or fanatic—or a "nut," as he put it. "It's just something I don't believe in."

"No." His mouth slanted in a crooked and amused line. "I don't suppose you believe in the Easter Bunny or the Tooth Fairy either."

"As a matter of fact, I don't." Her reply was unnecessarily sharp, but Tagg Williams didn't appear to notice.

"Holly and I would like you to come with us. When I get out the axe, you can look the other way," he suggested.

"Really, I don't—" Leslie started to repeat her refusal, but she was interrupted by her aunt.

"Forget all that tree business. It will do you good to be outside in the fresh air. It's just what you need after being cooped up so long," her aunt insisted in a mildly scolding tone. "Don't take any more arguments from her, Taggart. She'll go with you."

"Aunt Patsy." Leslie turned on her aunt, irritated that she had intervened.

"Now admit it, Leslie. You would enjoy being outside in the wood," she said in challenge.

That part of it did sound fun, Leslie had to admit it—if only to herself. She battled for a silent moment with her inner convictions and decided to take advantage of the opportunity to be outdoors. The dogsled was the ideal vehicle to accomplish it so she wouldn't have to rely on the dubious support of her crutches on ice and snow. Since she had already stated her views regarding so-called Christmas trees, she wasn't really compromising her position.

"I'll come," she agreed, then added, "—as long as you understand that I think what you're doing is wrong and a waste of a good tree. So don't ask me to help you pick one out."

"We won't." His smiling look gave Leslie the impression that he knew in advance she'd agree to come with them. "While you get your coat and scarf, I'll start the car and get it warmed up. We'll be ready to go in five minutes." He reached for the door to open it. "Don't change your mind." It was a warning against second thoughts.

"I won't." Leslie rarely backed off a decision once

she'd made it. She wasn't the type to waver or regret impulsive decisions.

A rush of cold, December air swept into the kitchen when Tagg departed via the side door. Leslie shivered in a reflexive action to the sudden chill. In addition to her winter coat and scarf, she'd need a ski hat and her furlined gloves—and a couple of wool socks for her bare toes.

# CHAPTER

3

HOLLY WAS IN perpetual motion in the front seat of the station wagon, too excited to sit still. Leslie had the entire back seat to herself, sitting sideways with her legs stretched over the seat and leaning against the locked, rear passenger door. The used dogsled was stowed on its side in the back, surrounded by the blanket robes so it couldn't slide all over.

"How much farther now, Daddy?" Holly wanted to know.

They were traveling down one of the many unpaved backroads that laced the rural countryside of Vermont. A brief snowfall the night before had coated mountain, tree, and valley with a pristine whiteness. It was a scene of picture-postcard perfection.

"It's the next farm just up the road," Tagg replied patiently to her oft-repeated question. He partially turned his head in Leslie's direction without taking his eyes off the road. "Abe Bellows gave us permission to take a tree from his woods."

"I wasn't going to accuse you of trespassing on someone else's property," she responded dryly.

"Come spring, he's going to brush-hog most of it so he can use it as a pasture for his dairy cattle," he informed her. "Most of the smaller trees will be cleared out of the valley area when that happens."

Leslie made no reply. She understood the reason Tagg was telling her this. He wanted her to know the tree they'd be cutting down for Christmas would be one that would be bulldozed out when the land was cleared the following spring. There was a degree of consolation in that knowledge, yet it didn't change the fact that she found this whole business of Christmas deplorably overdone.

Slowing the station wagon, he turned it into the farm lane already snow-packed from the comings and goings of other vehicles. There was a crunch of tires in the hard snow and the metallic rattle of chains with each rotation of the wheels.

A big collie came bounding out from a red barn

to announce their arrival and escorted them past the buildings to a far gate. It continued to bark when Tagg stopped the car, but its flag of a tail waved the air in a manner that seemed more friendly than threatening. The minute Tagg opened the driver's door, the dog was pushing its cold nose inside to have its head scratched.

"Some watchdog," Leslie laughed.

"He told everybody we were here, didn't ya, fella." Tagg rubbed its ears, then gently pushed it out of the way to step outside. "You might as well stay in the car until I get things unloaded."

"I'll help." Holly shot out of her side, certain her father wasn't talking to her.

Unless someone opened the rear door by her feet, Leslie had very little choice but to stay in the car. It wouldn't do any good to open the door she was leaning against because she couldn't possibly swing her left leg with its rigid cast around—and going out backward didn't exactly appeal to her. There wasn't any way she could reach the other door handle without a lot of wriggling and twisting. So she resigned herself to sit and wait until they had unloaded the things from the back.

Tagg lowered the tailgate of the station wagon and pulled the sled out. Holly was so busy playing with the brown and white collie that she forgot she had volunteered to help. Righting the sled, Tagg set it on its runners and tossed the fur robes onto it. Only two items remained in the back, an axe with its blade encased in a leather pocket and a leather rifle case. When he started to remove both, Leslie frowned in confusion.

"Why are you taking the rifle?" she asked, then arched a dryly mocking eyebrow. "Don't tell me you're going to shoot the tree before you chop it down."

"No," he chuckled, his warm breath turning into a vaporous cloud when it came in contact with the cold air. "I thought we might see some mistletoe while we're out."

"And you're going to shoot it?" That didn't make any more sense than her first question.

"Yes." His smile widened at the absolute confusion that took over her expression. "It's a parasitic plant that you usually see growing in the tops of other trees. There's only two ways to get it. You can either climb the tree or shoot the mistletoe out of it."

"You'd have to be a pretty good shot," Leslie declared.

"So I've heard," he replied with a deepening smile.

It was a crazy combination of arrogance and modesty. She laughed softly, in spite of herself. Tagg shut up the rear of the wagon and pushed the dogsled around the car to the fence gate. It was already standing open, so he took the sled on into the thickly wooded field.

Without the car's heater running, Leslie was beginning to feel the nipping cold of the winter afternoon. She lowered her chin so the wool scarf around her neck would cover more of her face and partly warm the air she breathed. Tagg was doing something to the sled, but she couldn't see too well since Holly and the frolicking dog had joined him. She glanced upward at the pearl gray sky overhead. It seemed to blend with the white snowscape that surrounded them.

When she heard footsteps approaching the station wagon, she pulled her gaze down. As Tagg walked back to the car, he pulled a ski cap out of his jacket pocket and covered his dark head with it. She reached down to pick up her crutches that were lying on the floor, then noticed Tagg was coming to the wrong side.

"Open the other door." She motioned to the one closest to her feet, but he gave no sign that he heard her. Half-turning, she rolled down the car window to repeat it. He reached through the opening and pulled the door lock. "Not this door," Leslie protested, but it was already swinging open behind her.

"You aren't going to need those crutches," Tagg

advised her and hooked an arm around the front of her waist.

"What are you doing?" She almost panicked when he began dragging her backward out of the car, but she had already guessed his intentions before he slipped a supporting arm under her legs. "You can't carry me—not with this heavy cast."

Instinctively she wrapped an arm around his neck to hold on and gripped at the ridge of his shoulder with her other hand, afraid he might suddenly drop her. When he had her free of both the car seat and the door, he straightened and threw her a little higher in his arms to get a firmer hold. Her heart seemed to catapult into her throat. He turned his face to her, his blue eyes lazy with amusement.

"I tell you what. If it looks like I'm going to drop you, I'll make sure you land in a soft snowdrift. How's that?" he mocked.

She was so close to him that she caught the lingering scent of the tangy aftershave lotion on his smoothly shaven jaw. The cold temperature had already begun to stiffen his mouth, limiting the movement of his lips as they formed the words. It was difficult to keep her gaze from straying to his mouth, only disturbing inches away from hers. Leslie tried to concentrate on what he said and stop this purely sexual attraction from holding sway with her. But it wasn't easy with the warmth of his breath trailing over her skin.

"You'd better make sure it's a soft snowdrift. One broken leg is bad enough." Her voice was husky with the inner disturbance of his nearness.

"I promise." He started toward the sled, carrying her in his arms with her left leg sticking rigidly and awkwardly in the air.

Although Tagg carried her with seeming ease, Leslie noticed the muscles standing out in his neck, which proved it was requiring no little effort. When he reached the sled, he dropped down on one knee and carefully set her on the furry robe draped over the sled and its backrest. The second robe he took and covered her with it, tucking in the sides.

His breath was coming quicker after the exertion of carrying her, but Leslie didn't think he was actually puffing. "Just think." This time, she was the one who had a mocking gleam in her eye. "Now you get to pull me."

"You aren't exactly a lightweight, are you?" An eyebrow lifted in laughing, good humor.

"Can I ride in the sled, too, Daddy?" Holly requested eagerly.

He paused, resting an arm on his bent knee, looked at his daughter, and mildly shook his head in a gesture of defeat. "You can ride for a little while," he agreed.

"Oh, goodie!" She clapped her hands together in excitement and jumped up and down. The dog began barking, certain this was some new game.

Tagg picked her up. "You have to be careful of Leslie's leg," he warned as he set her toward the front of the sled. "And you have to sit still. No bouncing around or you might overturn the sled. We didn't ask Leslie to come with us just to get hurt. Agreed?"

"Yes, Daddy." She sat primly still, mischief darting out of her blue eyes.

"If she gives you any trouble—" Tagg glanced at Leslie, "—just boot her into the snow."

"I will." Leslie snuggled deeper under the warm robe, burying her cold nose in the soft fur, and watched Tagg move to the front of the sled.

He'd rigged up some kind of a shoulder and chest harness to pull the sled. After he had shrugged into it, he adjusted the straps over the thickness of his wool coat. The collie sat forlornly beside the sled, whining at Holly and brushing at the snow with its tail.

"Can the dog ride in the sled, too, Daddy?" Holly couldn't resist the appeal of the dog's brown eyes.

"No. He's got four legs. He can run beside it." Tagg was definite in his refusal to haul another able-bodied passenger. As he leaned into the harness, the sled's runner glided cleanly through the few inches of new snow.

"Mush! Mush!" Holly ordered loudly and immediately began giggling. Leslie laughed, too, but she made sure hers was muffled by the robe.

"I'll 'mush' you," Tagg threatened, but there was a smile in his voice.

The ground fell away from the fence gate in a gentle, downward slope. It was relatively easy pulling the first forty yards until the land leveled out and became densely populated with trees. Then it became more of a trick maneuvering around them and finding a fairly straight path through them. The collie trotted alongside, sometimes dashing off to chase a squirrel or a rabbit, but always coming back.

The novelty of riding in the sled quickly wore off for Holly. The dog seemed to be having more fun than she was. "I wanta walk, Daddy. Stop the sled."

He halted so she could climb off, his breath running out in large white puffs. "Watch her leg," he warned Holly again, but she scrambled off the right side to avoid bumping Leslie's cast. His gaze lingered on Leslie, buried under the robe until only her eyes and part of her nose were showing. "Are you warm?"

"Yes." She nodded, in case he couldn't hear her muffled answer.

The briskness of the cold air sharpened all her

senses while the rest of her managed to stay warm and cozy under the robes. When Tagg began trudging onward again, Leslie relaxed and enjoyed the relatively smooth ride.

A blue jay flitted from tree to tree, following them through the woods and calling raucously to warn the other creatures of the humans' presence. There was hardly any breeze, but every now and then, its faint breath would blow at the clumps of snow on the skeletal branches of the maples and the birch and send crystalline flakes drifting downward.

Their trek was taking them down the length of a meandering and narrow valley, with mountains rising up on each side. There was a small stream running through, frozen over in places and running free in others. Sometimes they were close enough for Leslie to hear the musical tinkle of the water spilling over the rocks.

They were some distance from the fence gate when they finally reached an area where a stand of firs was growing at the base of the mountain. Tagg halted and shrugged out of the harness.

"We should be able to find a tree in that bunch," he said to Holly and walked to the sled for his axe. As he bent down, he winked at Leslie. "Be sure to look the other way when I start chopping."

She lowered the robe away from her mouth long

enough to say, "Are you afraid I'll start shouting 'Woodsman, spare that tree'?"

"I wouldn't be surprised." Tagg tried to smile, but the cold had stiffened his mouth. His eyes crinkled up at the corners instead.

As Leslie watched him walk away to the stand of pines, she wondered how she could joke about something she believed in so strongly. Maybe it was just that Tagg Williams made it difficult to be angry, and stay angry.

"Let's get this one, Daddy." Holly picked out a tree that was at least ten feet tall.

"It's too big. This one's more your size."

Their voices carried clearly across the snow. Leslie didn't have to strain to hear them. She couldn't see which tree Tagg had chosen, her view blocked by larger ones. It wasn't long before she heard the biting thud of the axe blade into a tree trunk. She looked away, not really to avoid the scene that was transpiring, but to assess the area. With fewer trees, more grass would grow in the valley to provide the farmer with pastureland for his dairy herd.

There was the splintering crack of wood giving way. Leslie tried to make it an abstract sound, not wanting anything unpleasant to intrude on this outing. She was enjoying herself and she was determined to continue enjoying herself.

The dog started barking. When she looked around, she saw Tagg dragging a small tree through the snow with the dog running alongside. The leather case was covering the axe blade he carried by its wooden handle. Holly broke away and ran toward the sled.

"Do you see our tree, Leslie? It's a pretty one, isn't it?" she declared excitedly.

Fortunately for Leslie, Holly didn't seem to expect a response, so she wasn't forced into a position of pretending or offending. Tagg noticed her silence, however, as he approached the sled.

"I'm afraid the tree is going to have to ride with you. I hope you don't mind too much," he said.

"It's all right."

He tied it onto the front part of the sled with a couple lengths of twine. It was a small, well-shaped tree, about four feet tall. The resinous smell of its needles scented the air Leslie breathed, making it pungently clean.

"Hold on," he advised her. "I'm going to turn the sled around."

Picking up the front runners, he held them just inches off the ground and used Leslie's weight at the back of the sled as an anchor point to make a slow pivot. With a few adjustments of the rear, he soon had the sled turned around and pointing in the direction they had come.

Before he strapped himself into the harness, he took the rifle out of its leather carrying case. "I saw some mistletoe along the way," he explained.

It was about a third of the way back along their trail. Before he took aim, Tagg pointed its location out to Leslie. It was growing on some of the highest limbs of the tree. Holly stood behind her father with her hands clamped over her ears and her eyes squeezed tightly shut.

Even though Leslie was prepared for it, she jumped involuntarily at the initial explosion of the first rifle shot. A squirrel scolded them in a loud, chattering voice from its perch in another tree. Its tirade nearly drowned out the sound of something falling through the tree limbs to the ground.

Holly and the dog went scampering through the snow to retrieve it, while Tagg waited until both were standing beside him before shooting again. After the third time, he removed the remaining bullets and started to slip the rifle into its case.

"But Daddy, there's more," Holly protested when she and the dog came running through the snow with the last sprig of mistletoe.

"We have all we need," he replied. "Put the mistletoe in the sack with the rest. It's time we were headed back to the car."

Leslie caught something in his tone of voice. It

was a full second before she realized the flakes of snow drifting in the air hadn't been blown from the trees. The temperature had warmed up a little and it had started to snow.

"Daddy, it's snowing!" Holly made the same discovery, and turned up a hand, trying to catch a flake in her mitten. "What if we get lost? What if it snows so hard we can't see to find our way back? We should have left pieces of bread like Hansel and Gretel did."

"I think the sled made some very plain tracks. If we follow them, I bet we'll find our way to the car," he replied dryly.

"Let's pretend the tracks aren't there. It'd be more fun," Holly insisted, wanting to taste a little thrill of adventure.

"Okay, you pretend." He glanced over his shoulder at Leslie. "And I'll follow the tracks."

There was something enchanting and magical about the return trip with lazy flakes spiraling down through the trees. All was quiet and hushed, except for the crunch of footsteps and the slicing sound the sled's runners made through the snow. It seemed much shorter going back to the car.

This time Tagg pulled the sled through the gate and right up next to the rear car door. He was breathing hard when he shrugged off the harness and came back to help Leslie out of the sled. The last stretch had been a steady uphill pull.

"If I tried to carry you this time, I probably would drop you," he admitted with a cold-stiffened grin, and helped her to stand up on her good leg, supporting her with an arm around the waist while he opened the car door to the rear seat. "Can you make it, or should I get your crutches?"

"I can make it." She grabbed hold of the door frame and made short little hops. Then she slid into the car backward, dragging her casted leg onto the seat.

Once he was sure she was safely inside, Tagg shut the door. It took a few minutes more to load the dogsled, the robes, and the tree into the back of the wagon. Holly hugged the collie goodbye for at least the fifth time and climbed into the front seat. Shuddering, Tagg slipped behind the wheel and pulled off his right glove to blow on his fingers.

"Now to get warm," he declared and started the motor with the ignition key.

By the time they drove out of the farmer's lane onto the backroad, warm air was blowing from the heat vents. The heat intensified the scent of pine needles in the air. It wasn't long before Holly became infected with the smell of the tree and broke into song, a loud if occasionally off-key rendition of "O Christmas Tree." Tagg joined in, and his voice was a rich baritone. Leslie sat silently in the backseat, feeling alone, unable to take part in this spontaneous joyfest of Christmas carols.

The singing ended when they turned into the driveway to the brick house next door to her aunt's. Tagg helped Leslie out of the car and passed her the crutches.

"Thanks for asking me to come along." She stood awkwardly on her crutches, aware that earlier she could have expressed herself with more genuine feeling behind the words. But the caroling had taken something away. "I did enjoy myself."

"You can't go home yet," he stated. "I wouldn't be much of a host if I sent you home without any refreshments. Come in and have some hot cocoa with us."

"I—" She was going to accept the invitation, but Holly seemed to think she wouldn't.

"Yes, do, Leslie." She grabbed at her hand to lend force to her plea. "Daddy makes the best cocoa you ever tasted, with lots of gooey marshmallows melting on top."

"All right, I'll come," she laughed. Her pleasure in the day had returned. Leslie couldn't sort through the reasons and come up with the right one, but it had something to do with being included, and sharing, of being a part of a whole. It didn't really matter as long as it felt good.

The living room was done in warm colors—cranberrys and golds with a smattering of orange. Richly grained maple woodwork was used throughout, including the staircase to the second floor. The house was comfortable and old and lived-in.

"Have a seat," Tagg invited, giving her the choice of the sofa or the matching chair with an ottoman.

Leslie chose the chair with the ottoman so she could rest her leg on it. When he started toward the dining room with the kitchen presumably beyond it, she asked quickly. "Would you like me to help you fix the cocoa?"

"Thanks, but I can manage," he refused with an easy smile.

"Look." Holly claimed her attention. "Over here is where we're going to put our tree. Right in front of the window. And when we turn on the lights at night, everyone who goes by can see it."

"That's true," Leslie agreed.

"Daddy and I finished the paper chain. Let me show you." She didn't wait to see if Leslie wanted to see it or not, and dashed off to another room.

Before Tagg brought the mugs of cocoa to the living room, Holly had an endless number of things to show Leslie. Some of them were

Christmas oriented and some were not. Leslie looked at all of them and listened patiently to the little girl's prattle.

"Has she talked your leg off yet?" Tagg asked as he handed Leslie a mug of cocoa with frothy, melted marshmallows floating on top.

"Almost," she smiled in understanding.

Holly immediately took a sip of her own cocoa and stretched the tip of her tongue way out, trying to reach the sticking ring of marshmallow on her upper lip. "I got a white mustache just like Santa Claus," she laughed.

"You certainly do. You'd better go get a napkin," Tagg advised. "And bring some back for us."

"Okay." She set her mug carefully down on a coaster, then took off at a run for the kitchen.

"Believe it or not, she wears down about nine o'clock every night," he said to Leslie.

"She's certainly full of life and energy," Leslie agreed. "She was right about your cocoa, too. It's delicious. I've never had an instant mix that tasted this good."

"It isn't instant." He leaned forward, as if he was telling her a secret. "I made it from scratch. You are drinking the real McCoy, with milk, cocoa, sugar— the works."

She felt she'd really put her foot in it this time.

"I . . . I'm sorry," she awkwardly laughed out the apology. "I just assumed—"

"I couldn't always cook. You should have tasted some of my first biscuits. They were harder than any bride could make." He smoothed over the situation by making light of it. "But like a bride, a father can learn to cook out of necessity, too."

"I guess so," she conceded and took another sip of her cocoa.

"Your aunt mentioned you work for a large advertising agency in New York." Tagg made the comment as Holly came racing back into the room and passed napkins around.

"I'm an assistant to the senior vice-president— which is a fancy way of saying I'm a glorified secretary," Leslie explained with a ruefully dry smile, and didn't mention that she earned a salary considerably higher than a secretary's. "I'm on a first name basis with the maître d's at the best restaurants in New York even though I've never eaten in one of them. And I know where you can get a suit cleaned in an hour—and the birthdays and anniversaries of my boss's children. But I don't make coffee."

"And you don't have to report for work until after the holidays?" The rising inflection of his voice turned the statement into a question.

"That's right," Leslie nodded and patted the hard

cast under her pant's leg. "My cast will be off by then."

"Seems to me, your boss missed a good bet." A smile was tugging at the corners of his mouth.

"Why?" Curious, Leslie tipped her head to the side, not following his meaning.

"It's rather obvious." There was a wicked glint in his blue eyes, dancing and mischievous. "If a man took a notion to chase a girl with a broken leg around the desk, it's a sure thing that she couldn't run very far or very fast."

She had a sudden vision of that scene with Tagg as the pursuer. Her heart seemed to do a funny little somersault against her ribs. The breath she drew in became lodged in her throat, making it difficult to laugh off his little scenario.

"Why would he want to chase her?" Holly frowned in bewilderment.

"To catch her, of course." He reached out and rumpled the top of his daughter's head, then his gaze swung back to Leslie with veiled intensity. "That's why every man chases a woman—and vice versa."

There was a message in his remark, a statement of his interest in her. It quivered through her nerve endings, but it was accompanied by little fingerlings of personal doubt. She didn't want to rush into something, only to discover she was in over her head. In her experience, it had proved wiser to test the water by stages and not jump in.

"What happens when he catches her?" Holly's curiosity was thoroughly aroused.

"That, little lady, is something you'll discover for yourself when you're older," Tagg dodged the question. "That's part of the fun of growing up."

Holly turned to Leslie, a somewhat bored look on her face. "I'll bet he kisses her. Bobby Jenkins is always trying to kiss me."

There was a second of stunned silence as their glances met above Holly's dark head. Tagg couldn't keep a short laugh from escaping his throat. "When I was her age, I was putting spiders down Lucy Vining's dress. They grow up quick nowadays."

The conversation shifted to less provocative topics. A half an hour later, Leslie had finished her cocoa and made excuses to leave. Tagg accompanied her the short distance to her aunt's house. A fine film of snow had collected on the steps, just enough to make the footing slippery, but it had stopped snowing.

With a crutch propping the storm door open, Leslie rested her weight on her good leg and one crutch and turned to thank Tagg for seeing her safely home. He was standing on the next to the top step.

"Thanks to you, I made it without one slip." She smiled.

"We'll be putting the tree up Sunday afternoon. Why don't you come over and help us?" he suggested.

"No thanks," Leslie refused with a quick shake of her head.

"You don't believe in Santa Claus and you don't believe in decorating Christmas trees." He shook his head at her in mock dismay.

"I just don't like anything associated with Christmas period," she admitted without apology. "There's nothing 'merry' about it."

"You're too young to be such a cynic," Tagg declared and stepped down a step. "I'm going to have to have a talk with Santa Claus."

"Sure," she laughed without humor. "And his flying reindeer, too." She pushed the inner door open and hopped inside before the storm door banged shut on her.

"Leslie?! Is that you?" Her aunt called from the living room.

"Yes, it's me. I'm back!" She balanced on her crutches and began taking off the layers of outer garments she'd worn for warmth.

Footsteps approached the kitchen in advance of her aunt's arrival. "I thought I heard the car drive in some time ago. Are you just getting back?"

"No. That was probably us you heard," Leslie

said and hopped over to a chair so she could take her snow boot off. "Tagg invited me in for cocoa."

An eyebrow was lifted at the ease with which she used his given name, but Patsy Evans made no comment on that. "Did you enjoy yourself?"

She thought about it a minute, then nodded. "Yes, I enjoyed myself." Oddly enough, it had been more fun than she had thought it would be.

"It isn't often that you meet someone who gets so much pleasure from their child," her aunt observed. "It's very heartwarming to see them together."

"I don't imagine it's easy for a man to be both father and mother," Leslie mused and tugged off her boot, tossing it onto the rug. A smile made a quick slant on her mouth. "Holly certainly isn't suffering any hardship having a bachelor father. Tagg is quite domestic. He made hot chocolate from scratch. That's something even I can't do."

# CHAPTER

## 4

SUNDAY MORNING AT Patsy Evans's house meant a late breakfast of pancakes with homemade Vermont maple syrup, sausages, and eggs. When the dishes were washed, Leslie took a cup of coffee into the living room and arranged herself in a chair with the Sunday newspaper spread around her to begin reading it section by section.

She was halfway through when she heard the floorboards creaking overhead. There was a brief moment of curiosity, certain her aunt had mentioned that she'd already made her bed. Then Leslie shrugged it aside and thought no more about it until she heard her aunt coming down the stairs.

Her eyes widened in mild surprise at the red pantsuit her aunt was wearing.

"Are you going somewhere?" Leslie asked.

"The local nursing home is having its Christmas program this afternoon. I volunteered to help with the refreshments. Didn't I mention it?" her aunt replied with an absent frown.

"No. Or, if you did, I'd forgotten."

"You're welcome to come with me," her aunt hurried to assure her of that.

"No, thanks, I'll stay here and read the paper." She turned down the invitation, which came as no surprise to her aunt.

"It will probably be close to six o'clock before I'm back." Her aunt slipped on her good coat with the dark mink collar and started for the kitchen. "Enjoy yourself."

"I will."

A few minutes after Leslie heard the side doors opening and closing, there was the muffled sound of an engine as a car reversed out of the driveway. The newspaper rattled companionably in the ensuing silence.

It didn't last long as a series of knocks loudly intruded. Leslie started to reach for her crutches, then guessed who it had to be. Since her aunt never locked the back door, she simply called out, "Come in!" Two sets of footsteps entered the kitchen, one light and one heavier. "I'm in the living room!" Leslie added.

Holly was the first to come dashing into the room, followed closely by Tagg Williams, his long strides making up for his slower pace. Holly leaned over the arm of Leslie's chair and claimed her attention.

"What are you doing?" she asked brightly.

"Reading the Sunday paper," Leslie stated the obvious, not needing to look at Tagg to be aware of the impact his presence made. He was standing a few feet away, his jacket unbuttoned to expose an ivory-colored sweater in a heavy ribbon-stitched knit.

"How are you with a needle and thread?" he asked.

The question momentarily threw her. "I can sew on a button. Why?"

"We need some help stringing popcorn and we thought we might be able to talk you into volunteering to give us a hand." There was a hint of a challenge in his look. "Have you got anything better to do on a Sunday afternoon?"

"I'm sure that's a matter of opinion," Leslie replied because she knew he wouldn't regard reading the paper as something better.

"Please, will you come over?" Holly added her plea. "Daddy's good at popping popcorn, but he's all thumbs with a needle."

"It's true," Tagg insisted with mock force and

held out his left hand, wagging his fingers. "I stuck myself twice with the needle already. Holly thinks it ruins the popcorn to have dots of blood on it."

Two flesh-colored bandages marked the wounded areas on his middle and forefinger. A tiny smile edged her mouth as she tried to picture someone as decidedly masculine as Tagg Williams pricking himself with a sewing needle.

"I know you're not into tree-trimming, but I've got a fire crackling in the fireplace, cocoa warming on the stove, and lots of popcorn to eat . . . or string, if you're more adept with a needle than I am." He grinned crookedly, making it very difficult for Leslie to resist his appeal.

"I'll help you," Holly promised. "It will go faster with both of us doing it."

"I can't believe I'm letting myself get talked into this," she declared on a laughing breath because she knew she was going to agree.

"Then you will help!" Holly realized with delight and spun away from her chair. "You were right, Daddy. You said she'd come."

Her side glance at Tagg held a hint of accusation along with a touch of droll amusement. "Did someone let the cat out of the bag?"

"Let's just say, I knew you'd take pity on a couple

of helpless souls." His darkly tanned features were gentled by the suggestion of a smile.

"I wouldn't be surprised if you poked yourself with the needle on purpose," Leslie accused, but without anger.

Tagg drew back in mock dismay. "Do I look like the kind of guy who would do something like that?"

"I don't think I'll answer that." The dryness in her voice was deliberate, indicating that he might be capable of such devious behavior.

"Here's your crutches." Holly gathered them up from where Leslie had them stored on the floor next to her chair. Now that Leslie had agreed to come, Holly was in a hurry for them to get under way.

Snowflakes were swirling out of a leaden sky as they crossed the driveway that separated the two houses. Woodsmoke was curling from the chimney of the Williams' house, its pungent odor being carried down by the heavy air. Holly was quick to point out the tree framed by the front window, but it was difficult to see beyond the reflection of the glass in the daylight.

Boxes of tree ornaments and tinsel garlands were strewn across the chair and matching ottoman in the living room. The sofa seemed to be the only piece of furniture that had escaped the litter of Christmas decorations. A huge bowl of popcorn was sitting at the coffee table in front of it, plus a six-inch-long strand of strung popcorn.

Balancing on first one crutch, then the other, Leslie took off her coat and passed it to Tagg to hang in the coat closet. She ran a hand through the length of her desert tan hair, trying to rid it of the static electricity that was making it cling to the green plaid sweater vest she was wearing.

"Daddy, can I plug in the tree lights so Leslie can see how nice it's going to look?" Holly was already beside the tree with the electric plug in hand.

"First you get a pillow for Leslie so she can prop her leg on the coffee table. Then you can plug in the lights," Tagg answered.

When she was comfortably settled on the sofa with her injured limb cushioned on a pillow, Holly plugged in the tree lights for Leslie to admire. After a few seconds, the white fairy lights began winking on and off in a haphazard pattern. Atop the tree, an aluminum star with a pale blue bulb shone down on the branches.

"It's very nice, Holly." Leslie had to make some comment for the child's sake, but Holly sensed her lack of enthusiasm.

"It will look lots better when we put the rest of the stuff on the tree," she insisted and wandered over to the sofa to sit down beside Leslie. "This is the popcorn string I started." She picked up the one lying beside the popcorn bowl. "I threw Daddy's away. That's his needle and string—what's left of it anyway."

"Shall we set the bowl between us and start in?" Leslie suggested.

"If you want to." But Holly sounded preoccupied, her mind on other things than stringing the popcorn. Almost dutifully she nestled the bowl of popcorn on the sofa between them and handed Leslie the unused needle and string.

Out of the corner of her eye, Leslie was aware of Tagg walking to the fireplace and bending down to poke the glowing red coals. Another split log was added. Flames sprang up to pop and snap over the fresh fuel. Leslie began spearing popcorn on the needle and pushing the bunches down the string.

"How come you don't like Christmas, Leslie?" Holly broke the short lull.

She flashed a quick glance at Tagg. He was watching her, but he gave no sign that he intended to jump in and field the question for her. Leslie hesitated, choosing her words carefully.

"It isn't that I don't like Christmas," she tried to qualify her aversion to the season. "It's all the fuss that goes along with it. It's the decorations and the gift-giving and all the meaningless things that go along with them. Too many people are making too much money off a day that's supposed to be a religious holiday. I guess I believe the meaning of Christmas has become lost under the fancy foil wrappings and bright ribbons."

"That's why you don't believe in Santa Claus, too." Holly seemed troubled by Leslie's failure to perpetuate the myth.

"Do you know what Christmas is?" Leslie didn't want to go into the business of Santa Claus. It wasn't her place to puncture the child's belief in that myth.

"It's the day Jesus was born. And we give presents to each other because the Three Wise Men brought gifts to the baby Jesus," she answered without hesitation. "Our Sunday School is going to have a Christmas program, telling the story of Baby Jesus being born in the manger because there was no room in the inn. I'm going to be one of the sheep that came with the shepherds. Sally Tuttle says I'm going to be a black sheep because of my hair. She gets to be the angel." Holly sighed at the unfairness of it.

"Black or white, you'll make a good sheep." Tagg straightened from his crouched position beside the hearth, joining the conversation.

"I don't mind being a sheep, 'cause I get to sit and watch everyone else." Holly made it clear that she wasn't bothered by the simpleness of her role in the pageant. "When you were a little girl, what did you do in your Christmas program?"

"I played the cow—and please—" she glanced wryly at Tagg as he approached the sofa, "—no comments from you."

"I was the inn-keeper who turned Mary and Joseph away," he said to prove his childhood role had been nothing to brag about. Reaching over, he scooped up a handful of popcorn.

"You aren't supposed to eat that, Dad," Holly scolded him. "It's for the tree."

"Sorry." Tagg crunched away at a half dozen popped kernels.

"Did you like Christmas when you were a little girl?" Holly was back on her previous subject.

"Mostly I think I liked all the presents under the tree," Leslie admitted.

"Did Santa bring them?"

She held her breath a second, trying to find a way to avoid the question and not lie. "My parents gave me most of them."

"It must be sad not to believe in the goodness of Santa Claus," Holly declared.

The phrasing of her response shook Leslie a little. She glanced at the child, jet black hair falling forward across her cheeks as she bent her head to the task of stringing popcorn. She longed to question what Holly had meant by believing "in the goodness of Santa Claus," but she didn't.

"Which do you want me to put on the tree next, Holly?" Tagg had moved to the armchair with its assortment of decorations. "The red garland or the gold one?"

"The red one." Holly tossed her partially strung strand of popcorn onto the coffee table and pushed off the couch. "I'll show you where I want it to go."

Although Holly lent a hand now and then, Leslie ended up stringing most of the popcorn. She had to admit it looked very pretty draped around the green boughs of the tree like some lacy white ribbon.

After the garlands of tinsel and popcorn came the shiny Christmas balls in a variety of colors and sparkling patterns. Tiny strips of tinsel added the finishing touch. Holly took part in the last with gay abandon, throwing handfuls at the tree. Almost as much landed on the floor and Tagg as stayed on the limbs.

"You've still got some tinsel in your hair." Leslie advised Tagg when he lowered himself onto the adjacent sofa cushion.

He combed his fingers through the thickness of his ebony dark hair, raking out the short pieces of tinsel. There was a wry light in his blue glance, warm with humor.

"I have the feeling we're going to find tinsel in everything," he murmured.

"She did get rather carried away," Leslie agreed and half-turned to glance over the sofa's back at his daughter. She was sitting cross-legged on the floor in front of the lighted Christmas tree.

Her elbows were propped on her knees to support her chin on her hands while Holly gazed at the glittering sight before her. The solid overcase beyond the front window pane had brought a premature darkness to the late afternoon sky. The clear glass reflected the winking lights of the tree, creating a magical scene.

"I think it's just beautiful," Holly sighed with theatrical exaggeration.

"It's the most beautiful Christmas tree I've ever seen," Tagg agreed with tongue in cheek, then looked around the room. "The stockings are hung by the fireplace . . . with care. The nativity scene is on the mantel. The wax carolers are adorning the dining room table. All the decorations are out. All that's left is for a little girl named Holly to clean up the mess."

"Ahh, Daddy, not now," she protested in a wheedling voice.

"Yes, now." He remained firm under the coaxing appeal of her dark blue eyes. "Put all the boxes and packages in the closet. When you're done, we'll have some cocoa."

"All right," Holly gave in grudgingly and rolled to her feet with an agility that only the young seemed to possess.

"There's a bright spot to all this," Leslie said above the background noise Holly was making as she stacked the smaller boxes inside larger ones.

"What's that?" Tagg tipped his head back to rest it on the top edge of the sofa. He rolled it to one side to look at her.

"In three weeks, you can take it all down and put it away until next year," she teased.

"Don't remind me." He faked a groan and shut his eyes with seeming weariness. "I haven't recovered from chopping down the tree, so I can't say I'm looking forward to hauling it out."

"Your muscles are stiff, hmm?" Leslie guessed.

"I wonder why," Tagg murmured dryly. "It couldn't be because I pulled you on that sled for nearly two miles, plus chopped down the Christmas tree."

"You left out the part where you carried me from the car to the sled," she reminded him.

"That's right," he remembered, thick lashes sweeping up to let his blue eyes study her again. "A really good secretary would be an expert at shoulder and neck massages. I've had a hard week. Why don't you give me a good rubdown?"

"Sorry. I draw the line at coffee and a massage."

Her refusal was brightly casual and offhand, but the hint of intimacy in his probing gaze made her feel anything but casual inside.

"I have the feeling that's not the only time you draw the line," Tagg said with a throaty chuckle.

"Hey, Dad! Look!" Holly cried excitedly from behind the couch, rattling a paper sack. "We don't have all the decorations up."

There was only so far Leslie could turn without moving her rigidly braced leg. Her head was turned as far to the side as it would go, but all she could see of Holly was her arm resting on the back of the sofa. The girl was evidently standing directly behind her. Something made Leslie glance at Tagg. His gaze was locked on a point a few inches above her head. She looked up and saw the sprig of mistletoe Holly was dangling above her.

"Now you've got to kiss her, Dad," Holly challenged with a giggling laugh.

"That's right, I do," he agreed.

Before Leslie could react, he was leaning toward her. Her pulse skipped a few beats when she found herself gazing into the black centers of his eyes. Her glance lowered to the strong, smooth line of his mouth, coming steadily closer. Her lashes came down a second before she felt the fanning warmth of his breath and the light pressure of his mouth so briefly touching hers.

It was over almost before it began. She blinked in vague surprise, feeling cheated. Which was silly since she'd always said that the business about kissing under the mistletoe was ridiculous.

There wasn't any time to assimilate her reaction or her response. Something was going on above and behind her. Tagg had grabbed his daughter's wrist and taken the spring of mistletoe away from her. He was moving back to his own side of the sofa, dragging Holly with him. The little girl was convulsing with laughter and he was smiling broadly. He held the mistletoe over his own head.

"Now you have to kiss me," he informed his daughter.

Laughing, Holly leaned across the back of the sofa and gave him a loud smack on the lips. Only then, did he let go of her. She disappeared behind the sofa and popped back up with the sack of mistletoe in hand.

"Where are we going to hang this, Daddy?" She wanted to know.

"I have no idea." Tagg opened the sack to drop the sprig into it. "Just put it up for now. We'll find a place for it later."

"I'll put it on the coffee table so we won't forget it again," Holly decided.

"I'll get the cocoa." Tagg pushed off the sofa and headed toward the kitchen.

Just like that, the incident was over and forgotten—or so it seemed to Leslie. A kiss that hadn't been a kiss at all, leaving no lingering awkwardness or sense of unease. It was just as if it had been too unimportant to dwell on. At least that appeared to be Tagg's attitude. Leslie discovered she couldn't dismiss it so easily.

With Holly around, there wasn't any lack of conversation while they drank their cocoa. When Tagg turned on a lamp beside the sofa, Leslie realized how late it was.

"I'd better be getting back. It's almost six and I didn't leave any note telling Aunt Patsy I'm here." Leslie reached for the crutches propped against the side of the sofa.

"It's been snowing. I'll walk over with you in case the steps are slick," Tagg volunteered, and started for the coat closet.

"Thanks for coming over and helping us." Holly hovered close by while Tagg helped Leslie into her coat.

"It was fun—and you have a lovely tree." The last was added as an afterthought, but she meant it. This time it wasn't an empty compliment.

As they went out the door, Tagg paused long

enough to tell his daughter, "I won't be gone long. If you get bored, you can wash the cocoa mugs." There was no response from Holly as he shut the door. "She's at the age where she thinks washing dishes is a treat. I'm sure she'll grow out of it."

"Everybody does," Leslie agreed with a quick smile. The snow had melted from the steps, but there were patches of ice and snow mixed in the driveway.

"Even though I'm prejudiced in her favor, I think Holly is turning into a little lady," he said with a degree of pride, then glanced at Leslie when she remained silent. "What? No comment?" he mocked.

"I was just thinking." She started not to tell him, then changed her mind. It was something she had observed and she was curious about it. "Holly never talks about her mother."

When Tagg came to an abrupt halt, Leslie stopped, too, wondering if she had unwittingly brought up a highly sensitive subject. A disturbing light had darkened his eyes; their gaze was centered on her as a profoundly pleased expression stole across his ruggedly handsome features.

"Well, well." It was a lowly voiced expression of satisfaction. "It's about time."

"I beg your pardon?" Her hazel eyes scanned his face in confusion, bathed in the light thrown from the windows of his house. The subdued light highlighted his angular features, emphasizing their planes and hollows.

"You've finally asked about Holly's mother." Again his voice was ringed with satisfaction. She noticed the faint deepening of the grooves etched into his tanned cheeks that indicated a suppressed, but dimpling smile.

"I don't understand." Leslie shook her head slightly in vague bewilderment. "Was I supposed to ask about her before or what?"

"Not necessarily." He spread his hand across her back to begin guiding her again toward her aunt's home. "It's just that when a woman asks about a man's past, it usually means she's interested in his future."

"I was asking because of Holly," she responded quickly, which was partially true—but only partially.

"Of course." His voice dryly mocked out an agreement. "It isn't too surprising that Holly doesn't talk about her. Cindy—my wife—died a month after Holly was born, so Holly has no memory of her."

"What happened?" Since he didn't appear to object to talking about his wife, Leslie went ahead and asked the question.

"There were complications in the delivery; infection set in; then pneumonia." It was a very clinical explanation with no insight into how his wife's death had affected him.

Leslie made a tactful attempt to probe into that area. "It must have been a difficult time for you—losing your wife and having a newborn baby to take care of and raise."

"Yes." It was a detached admission that lost even more of its credibility when he slanted a dry smile in her direction. "But Holly and I managed to survive it without any lasting damage. Although—" Tagg paused and briefly lifted his gaze skyward in a thoughtful attitude. "I guess a person never stops wondering what might have happened if things had turned out differently."

Which meant what? That he still longed for his wife? Did he think his life would be better or worse, if she had lived? It was impossible to come to a conclusion either way. His remark hadn't revealed enough. Leslie shied away from delving into something that was so personal.

As they reached the steps to the side door, Tagg moved in front of her to take the lead. "I'll turn the lights on for you."

By the time she mounted the steps, he had the doors opened and the kitchen light turned on. Tagg waited inside for her and helped remove her coat, an awkward task when one had to balance on crutches. For the time being, Leslie draped her coat over the back of a kitchen chair, then turned back to him. He stood on the large rug, his hands thrust into the pockets of his open jacket.

The gesture of her hand as it brushed her silky, sand-colored hair away from the side of her face was almost a self-conscious one. His features were relaxed in a warm smile, but they didn't mask the inner probing of his gaze on her.

"I know a tree-trimming party is not your idea of fun, but I hope it didn't turn out to be too much of an ordeal," he said.

"It didn't." As a matter of fact, this was the second time she had enjoyed taking part in a Christmas-type activity. Perhaps she'd simply had too many bad memories associated with Christmas and not enough happy ones to offset them.

"I meant to apologize for Holly's behavior. I hope she didn't embarrass you with that mistletoe incident." The curve of his mouth increased, taking on a rueful line in the rest of his expression. "I noticed you didn't look too pleased about it."

"I didn't?" Leslie hadn't thought it showed. "I've always regarded kissing under the mistletoe to be a silly tradition. It's forced on both parties whether either one wants it or not."

"It can be a useful ploy sometimes when a man

wants to kiss a woman and he hasn't been given the opportunity. But, as you say—" he lifted a shoulder in a vague shrug, "—it doesn't necessarily mean the lady is willing. She could be just tolerating it. I suppose that's happened to you."

"More times than I care to count." It was one of the reasons she'd sworn off office Christmas parties.

"Was today one of them?" Tagg asked and immediately widened his smile. "That's a leading question, isn't it?"

"Very leading," she agreed with a self-conscious laugh. A warmth was beginning to spread through her veins and heat her skin until she felt slightly flushed.

"I guess you know where it's leading, too." He withdrew his hands from his pockets and took a step closer, reaching for her waist. Their touch just seemed to add to the warmth already coursing through her. His glance flicked upward, above her head, then down to hold her gaze. "There's no mistletoe—no obligation to kiss or be kissed."

"No," Leslie agreed, feeling oddly breathless in anticipation.

When he began bending his head toward her, he blocked out the overhead light. In an automatic response, her chin lifted. His mouth settled onto hers with natural ease, its warmth melting away the little hesitancy that remained. Her lips moved against his, liking the stimulating feel of them.

His arm slid to the back of her waist, taking more of her weight so she had to rely less on the crutches for support. With his other hand, he took first one, then the other away from her and set them against the kitchen counter. Her hands found a way inside his jacket and circled his middle as he gathered her more fully into his arms.

A heady pleasure was building inside her as his mouth continued to roll over her lips, exploring their softness and inciting their response. That tangy fragrance clinging to his skin filled her senses with each deepening breath she took. His hands made a slow foray over her shoulders and back, traveling over the curve of her spine and shaping her to his length. Leslie was distantly conscious of his flatly muscled build, and the heat his body generated combining with hers.

When he ended the kiss, the moist heat of his breath continued to warm her lips. No attempt was made by either to pull back and increase the distance between their lips. Through the veiling screen of her lashes, Leslie studied the firm line of his chin and the attractive grooves that flanked his mouth. She was conscious that his breathing was disturbed, not coming as evenly as it normally did.

She knew her pulse was racing wildly, indicating the kiss had a similar, stimulating effect on her.

"I've been wanting to do that." His husky voice was pitched just above a whisper. It seemed to vibrate through her.

Lights flashed on the kitchen window as a car turned into the driveway. "That must be Aunt Patsy." Leslie reluctantly loosened her circling arms to draw away from him. "You'd better hand me my crutches."

"Children and relatives; they don't have the best timing," Tagg declared dryly and kept a supporting arm around Leslie while he reached for her crutches. "Holly with her mistletoe this afternoon and your aunt arriving at this particular moment."

"She could have come home sooner." She slipped the crutches under her arms and shifted a small distance away from him.

"The cynic sounding like Pollyanna?" Tagg mocked that she had found something good in the intrusion.

"Even Scrooge had his moments," Leslie retorted, hearing the slam of a car door.

"Which reminds me," he said. "Holly goes to school in the mornings. One day this next week, I planned to drive into Montpelier. Would you like to ride with me and keep me company while Holly's in school?"

"Don't tell me. Let me guess," she said. "You're going Christmas shopping."

He laughed silently. "Clever girl. How did you figure that out?"

"It just seemed logical. So far I've gone along when you went hunting for your tree. You asked me over to help trim it. So the only thing missing is the presents to be put under the tree," Leslie concluded.

"Most of my Christmas shopping is done, but I do have a couple of items yet to buy. I promise I won't drag you through all the toy departments. We'll have brunch somewhere before we come home." He arched an inquiring eyebrow. "Will you come?"

"Yes." It didn't seem necessary to add more than that.

"I'll pick a day when the weather's nice and let you know," he said.

"All right," Leslie nodded.

When the storm door was opened from the outside, Tagg pivoted and opened the inner door for her aunt. Patsy Evans looked momentarily surprised to see him, then recovered with her usual aplomb.

"Hello, Taggart," she greeted him with a curious look. "Was there something you wanted?"

"No. I was just making sure Leslie got in safely. I have to be getting back. I left Holly at the house alone." He excused himself and moved to exit through the door Patsy Evans had just entered.

"I saw your Christmas tree when I drove in. It looks beautiful," she stated.

"I'll tell Holly you said so," Tagg smiled, then nodded to Leslie. "I'll see you."

When the door closed behind him, Leslie realized her aunt was watching her. She turned and Patsy busily began taking off her coat.

"I'm glad you didn't have to spend the afternoon alone," she commented.

"I helped string popcorn to hang on the tree," Leslie explained.

"I must say I like the way Taggart does things— going out and chopping down his own Christmas tree, encouraging his daughter to make things to hang on it." Her aunt elaborated on her initial comment.

"Yes." Leslie moved over to the sink. "Shall I heat some water for tea?"

"Sounds good. Please."

"By the way—" she held the teakettle under the faucet and began filling it with water, "—he is a widower. His wife died of complications from childbirth a month after Holly was born."

"Really?" Her aunt appeared vaguely surprised by the news. "Somehow I had the feeling he was divorced. Not that it really matters." Her shrewd glance ran keenly over Leslie. "It was thoughtful of him to see you home."

"Yes." She hobbled over to the stove to put the kettle on to heat. "Some morning this next week, he asked me to ride into Montpelier with him."

"Are you going?"

Leslie turned, her eyes widening slightly at the question. "I thought I would, yes. Why?"

"No reason." Her aunt shrugged. "I guess I was just wondering whether this was the start of a holiday romance."

Her mouth opened to refute the idea, then closed without saying a word. It probably would turn out to be a short-lived relationship. It would be foolish to think that this time would be different from any of the others in the past.

# CHAPTER

## 5

THE GOLD DOME of the granite Capitol Building glinted in the morning sunlight. A snow-covered, wooded hillside rose abruptly behind it to form an appropriately rural backdrop for the white statue of Ceres, the Roman Goddess of agriculture, standing atop the glittering gold dome.

There was little traffic on the street as Tagg drove by the State House. Leslie's gaze was drawn to the statue of Ethan Allen, standing proud and tall on the front portico of the Capitol Building, his arm upraised. This famed leader of Vermont's Green Mountain Men seemed to be standing guard over the independence they had battled to win from Britain, an independence Vermont had retained for fourteen years before finally joining the Union formed by the original thirteen.

"Small but impressive, isn't it?" Tagg noticed her interest in the Vermont State House and commented on it.

"Yes." Its size wasn't imposing, but there was a quiet majesty in its classic architecture and a solid strength about its granite walls.

"It always fascinated me when I was growing up. I often wondered whether my perspective as an adult would change that, but it hasn't," he stated.

"Are you from Vermont?" Leslie ran her glance over his profile. It was a piece of information she didn't recall her aunt mentioning.

"Yes, I grew up here." His attention remained on the street they were traveling, watching the intersections and glancing at the businesses. "Then I left for college, and came back only once or twice since." His gaze flicked briefly to her, absently amused. "Don't I look like a crusty native to you?"

"No." Although she conceded that Tagg had retained that air of reserve even if it was behind a smiling mask. "Did your work bring you back?" It was a probing question since he didn't appear to do any kind of work.

"No." The answer was accompanied by a brief, negative movement of his head, but he didn't seem to regard her question as prying into his personal affairs. "It was time for Holly to start attending school on a regular basis—and I guess I wanted her to grow up in the kind of background I did. How about yourself?" A traffic light turned red and he slowed the car to a stop, sliding a glance at her. "Are you from New York—or somewhere else?" And Leslie realized that she didn't know any more about what he did for a living than she had before.

"I was born and raised right in Manhattan," she answered his question while she tried to think of a tactful way to ask her own again.

"Then you're a city girl." The light changed to green and Tagg started the car smoothly forward.

The faintly mocking tone of his remark made Leslie add, "I've never thought of myself as a city girl. My parents had a house on Fire Island so we usually spent the summers there. In the winter, we'd go skiing—sometimes here to Vermont and visit Aunt Patsy. So I had a blend of citylife and countrylife, until the divorce changed things."

"Your parents moved away from New York after they split up?" he asked if that's what her remark meant.

"Eventually," she nodded and huddled into her coat, not from the cold since the car's heater kept the interior warm. Mainly Leslie was withdrawing from unpleasant memories. "Both of them remarried. Dad and his new family live on the West Coast; and Mom and her family live in Baltimore. 'And never the twain shall meet,' as the saying goes." The last was issued with a certain rawness.

"It was a bitter divorce," Tagg guessed by her tone.

"It was a more bitter marriage." She shrugged, trying to make believe neither had mattered.

"Do you see them very often?"

"Not any more than I have to," Leslie admitted dryly. "I'm the spoils of their war, so they're both still fighting to claim me as theirs alone. And I don't like being the rope in a tug of war. That's why I came to stay with Aunt Patsy."

"I'm glad you did." Tagg smiled at her briefly, then noticed the store just ahead on the right. "There's where we're going—and there's an empty parking place out front. We're in luck."

There wasn't an opportunity for Leslie to turn the conversation back around and question Tagg about his occupation. So she had to bury her curiosity for the time being while he did his Christmas shopping.

Over an hour later, they returned to the car with his purchases made. Tagg stowed the brightly wrapped and ribboned packages in the back seat of the car, then held her crutches while Leslie maneuvered into the front passenger seat.

"And now to find someplace to eat," he declared as he slipped behind the wheel and took the car keys out of his pocket. "Hungry?"

"Just starting. I cheated and had toast and jam this morning," she confessed.

"So did I." Tagg chuckled softly, his glance moving over her. As he turned the car onto the street, he said, "I think I've figured out why you pretend not to like Christmas. It gives you a perfect excuse not to go through all this rigamarole of buying presents for people."

"Wrong." She laughed. "I just don't wait until the last minute to do all my shopping. My parents insist on giving me gifts—and a few of my friends. So I'm blackmailed into buying presents for them."

"A lot of people are too proud to accept a gift in the spirit that it's given," Tagg replied in understanding, then winked at her. "Of course, that's where Santa Claus steps in. How can a person say no to Santa Claus? He combines the joy of giving with the joy of receiving."

"I suppose that's true." Leslie leaned back in her seat to mull over that perspective of the Santa Claus myth.

The restaurant Tagg picked was relatively empty of customers. It was too early for lunch and the coffee break crowd had already left to return to work.

So their service was quick and their food was hot. After the waitress had cleared away their dishes, she refilled their coffee cups.

Leslie noticed Tagg glance at his watch to check the time. "Is it getting late?"

"No. Holly won't be getting out of school for another hour. We'll be able to take our time driving back," he assured her.

There was a stirring of activity at the restaurant entrance, the relative quiet disturbed by the arrival of a small group of businessmen meeting for lunch. The distraction brought a lull to their conversation as the hostess led them to a table. One of the men, a white-haired gentleman still in the prime of health, spied Tagg and immediately broke away from the group.

"As I live and breathe, if it isn't Tagg Williams," he declared and grabbed Tagg's hand to shake it before Tagg could stand up. "I didn't know you were back in these parts. How are you, son?" The man didn't wait for a response as he turned a twinkling look at Leslie. "What pretty lady are you romancing this time?" He reached across the table to shake Leslie's hand and introduce himself. "The name's Kyle Clarehorn. I'm an old friend of Tagg's family. And who might you be? I have to ask because he'll never tell me your name. He's afraid I'll steal you away, that's why."

"Leslie Stiles." She was half-surprised that she

was being given the chance to answer, but the man had to draw a breath sometime. His greeting had turned into a non-stop spiel. She was both amused and amazed at his energy, considering he was probably seventy if he was a day.

"Fine-looking woman, but you always did know how to pick them," he informed Tagg with an admiring shake of his head. Again, he split his attention to Leslie. "Better watch your step with this guy. Every time I see him, he's with a different lady. He draws them like flies to maple syrup."

"Holly has already warned me about him," Leslie assured him on a laughing note.

"Holly?" The name threw the white-haired gentleman for a moment.

"My daughter." Tagg pulled his keen glance from Leslie long enough to jog the man's memory.

"Your daughter, of course." He snapped his fingers in a gesture of self-impatience for forgetting. "How is that blue-eyed little charmer? It must be three years since you stopped by with her to visit. Cute as a button, she was. I'll bet she's got a long list made out for Santa Claus."

"Not a long one," Tagg replied. "But she's got a dog at the top of the list. Thankfully she's old enough to know that when she *asks* Santa for something, it doesn't necessarily mean she's going to get it."

"Every child should have a dog," the man insisted. "You tell Santa I said so. You couldn't pick a better Christmas present to teach a child the true meaning of love. Try spelling *dog* backward once. It's *god*. And if you think about it, a dog is always sad when you leave it and happy when you come back—never asking where you were in between—just as long as you come home. You make sure Santa brings that girl a dog," he ordered. "I wish I had time to stay and chat, but I have clients waiting." With a wink at Tagg and a hand gesture at Leslie, he said, "Better hang on to this one."

In the same flurry of energy that he had descended on them, the man was departing to rejoin his group. Leslie felt slightly out of breath, and the elderly man had been the one who did all the talking.

"He's quite a character," Tagg declared wryly.

"You can say that again," Leslie agreed.

"What did you mean when you said Holly had warned you about me?" His gaze narrowed on her with sharp curiosity.

"Oh that." Leslie tried to shrug it away, but realized he would persist until she explained. "She told me that all the girls fall in love with you and wondered if I would, too."

"I'm going to have to talk to that girl," Tagg declared in mild exasperation. "Between her and

Kyle, they're making me sound like a regular ladykiller."

"Aren't you?" she chided to get his reaction.

"Why would anybody want to be labeled a ladykiller or a playboy?" he reasoned. "The first implies that you kill ladies and what man would want a dead woman on his hands? And a playboy might have spent a lot of time in the company of the female sex, but I doubt if he's ever known one woman well."

"And you feel that's important?" Her voice was soft. Something inside her was waiting for his answer.

"You can't love an object, but you can love a person." Tagg reached for his coffee cup, breaking the intangible spell that had led them both into a topic with such underlying seriousness. "There's supposed to be a full moon Friday night, providing the sky is clear. How would you like to go on a sleigh ride with Holly for a chaperone?"

Leslie followed his lightning change of mood, arching a light brown eyebrow. "Jingle bells in a one-horse open sleigh?"

"You've got it," he grinned.

"I came here to escape all the Christmas hokum and I'm being deluged with it instead," she decried in mock protest.

"Bah humbug," Tagg mocked. "Even Scrooge was

converted into a believer. And I don't think you're as tough as he was."

"Is that right?" Leslie didn't attempt to deny it. Her position was steadily being undermined.

"Are you game for the sleigh ride, weather permitting?" he asked.

"Why not?" Her shoulders were lifted in a helpless shrug of mock defeat.

Tagg finished his coffee and glanced at Leslie as he set his empty cup on the table. "Are you ready to start for home?"

The ride back began in a companionable silence with Leslie gazing out the window at the picturesque countryside. The mountain state was sparsely populated, consisting of mainly valley farms, quaint villages, and small cities. The winter snows had given the rolling and wooded hillsides a serenely peaceful look, slumbering restfully to prepare for spring's burst of green growth.

As the road curved past a farmhouse, Leslie noticed a man out back, chopping wood. The sight turned her thoughts to her curiosity about Tagg's occupation. Candor seemed her only hope in obtaining an answer.

"What kind of work do you do?" Her sudden question after such a long silence seemed to briefly startle him.

As his attention swung back to the road, the side of his mouth was lifted up by a smile. "At the moment, none," he replied dryly. "I have a law degree and I'll probably open an office here after the first of the year. My father was a District Court Judge for a number of years before he died. I'm finally getting around to following in his footsteps."

"But what did you do before now?"

"I was a professional skier. Unlike golf or tennis pros, professional skiers are a relatively unknown breed. Unless a skier has competed in the Olympics, which I didn't, the public generally never hears about him. So don't be embarrassed because you've never heard of me," Tagg said as if he knew Leslie was trying to remember if she had heard his name before.

"I admit I haven't," she said.

"Mostly I competed on the European circuit. That's how I met Cindy. She was the daughter of one of my sponsors," he explained with no expression showing on his face. "After we were married, she discovered the skiing circuit wasn't the glamorous life she thought it would be. Two years later, we separated. I didn't know she was pregnant until a mutual friend told me before a meet in Grenoble. I flew to Colorado to see if we couldn't work things out. That was in November, and Holly was born the day after Christmas that year. You know the rest of the story."

"Is that when you quit skiing?" Leslie quietly studied him, realizing now how his skin had become so darkly tanned from the constant exposure to the glare of sun and snow and why he was in such superb physical condition when many men in their thirties were developing paunches.

"Not right away. Initially I only entered competitions in the Rocky Mountain area so I could keep Holly with me most of the time. When you compete, you have to go all out every time. You can't worry about accidents or injuries. Suddenly I couldn't do that, because I had Holly. I never felt like that when I got married; but I suppose I knew Cindy was old enough to take care of herself. Holly needed me, especially with Cindy gone. My present to her on her third birthday was to hang up my racing skis, and buy a resort in the Colorado mountains."

"Then you sold it and came back here to Vermont," Leslie guessed.

"That's about the size of it," he agreed. "It was a good business, but it didn't give me enough time to spend with Holly." His shoulder lifted in an idle shrug. "Maybe I just got burnt out on skiing. I have no more desire to be on the slopes. Maybe that will change someday and I'll enjoy the sport of it again."

"In the meantime, you're going to practice law."

"I enjoyed studying law," Tagg told her. "I suppose

the skiing interlude in my life was part of the wild oats I needed to sow. I don't regret it. It gave me Holly and sufficient funds to know that her future will be secure if anything happens to me." He flashed her a white smile. "And there you have my life story, my credentials, and even a glimpse at my bankbook."

"Was I being nosey?" She hadn't thought so. But most of the information, he had volunteered.

"No." He reached for her hand and threaded his fingers through hers. "I think you have the right to know something about the man who asked you out for a sleigh ride."

"That's true. I couldn't go sleigh riding with a total stranger," Leslie responded with the same bantering lightness he had used.

"I should hope not," Tagg mocked, then glanced at his wristwatch. "Everything is turning out perfectly this morning. I'll be able to take you to your aunt's, get the presents hidden in the house, and still have time to pick up Holly."

"That's good."

"I thought so, too." He squeezed her hand affectionately, a warm sensation spreading through her.

In the lull that settled, Leslie thought over the things Tagg had told her about himself, his life and his previous career in professional sports. It started her thinking about the comment Holly had made.

"When you were skiing, I imagine you had all sorts of beautiful women for company. I suppose that's where Holly got the idea that girls always fell in love with you." The minute she made the comment, she regretted it. "Now, I am being nosey. You don't have to answer that."

"I don't mind." He smiled at her briefly, letting his glance leave the road for a scanning second. "I didn't lack for female company, but I wouldn't go so far as to say there was an endless bevy of beauties. But it was the glamour of the ski slopes that attracted them— like Cindy. I doubt if it would have mattered to some of them if I was five feet tall with a receding hairline."

But he was six feet tall and unconventionally handsome. Leslie wasn't fooled. Those vital statistics had increased the attraction of the members of the opposite sex for him. She had no illusions about her own sex. Some were positively brazen in their pursuit of a man—single or not. She suspected the attentions of other women might have been one of the reasons for his marriage to go bad.

When they arrived at her aunt's house, Tagg parked the car in the driveway. "Do you need some help getting out?" he asked as she gathered up her unwieldy crutches.

"No, I can manage."

"I'm glad you came with me today." His hand

lightly fitted itself to the curve of the back of her neck, holding it while he leaned across the seat and kissed her with lingering force.

Leslie was conscious of the triphammer beat of her heart when she finally opened the car door. Her lips could still feel the warm pressure of his mouth. It was a decidedly pleasant sensation.

He waited until she had reached the door and turned to wave to him. Then he reversed out of the drive to pick up his daughter from school.

# CHAPTER

# 6

THE BAY MARE tossed its head in a show of eagerness, jingling the bell strap on its harness, but the horse stood calmly while Tagg lifted Leslie into the shiny black sleigh with its red leather seats. The fur robes that had kept her warm on the dogsled ride were folded on the seat.

"Where on earth did you find this horse and sleigh?" she asked in amazement. "It's something out of a Currier and Ives print."

"The horse and sleigh belong to a local farmer. He usually rents them out for the winter through the ski resorts in the area," he explained and swung Holly into the sleigh, then climbed in himself to sit between them. The fur robes were spread out lengthwise to cover all three of them against the numbing chill of the night air.

"Are we going to go 'dashing through the snow,' Daddy?" Holly was bouncing on the seat, unable to sit still.

"Not unless the snow is on the road," Tagg informed her dryly, just in case she had visions of them racing across some meadow.

Picking up the reins, he lightly slapped the horse's rump with them and clicked his tongue to signal the mare forward. There was a slight jerk, then the sleigh was pulling smoothly onto the snow-packed dirt road.

A huge silver-dollar moon gleamed brightly on the white ground and highlighted the snow clinging on dark tree branches. It was a magical wonderland of sight and sound, muted bells jingling in rhythm to the horse's trotting hooves. The cold air was sharp and invigorating and rosied Leslie's cheeks as she sat shoulder to shoulder with Tagg, unconsciously snuggling closer to his body warmth. Her hands and arms were buried under the thick, furry robe that insulated them against most of the frigid air.

"Let's sing, Daddy," Holly suggested.

"Let's don't," he replied. "Mr. Grey told me the horse stops every time people start singing."

"Smart horse." Leslie murmured *sotto voce*.

Holly leaned forward to look her father square in the eye, skeptical and challenging. "Is that true?"

"No," Tagg admitted. "But let's spare the horse's ears anyway."

"Okay." She sat back in her seat and hugged the fur robe around her chin.

All was quiet and still around them as they traveled down the back road. It didn't seem to matter where Leslie looked, some nostalgically familiar scene would leap out at her, painting a picture that she was certain she'd seen before. Whether it was the glitter of the moonlight on a meadow of snow or a farmhouse with lights shining from the window and smoke curling out of the chimney.

Tagg's hand found hers under the robe and curled around it. His head tipped slightly towards her. "Are you having fun—jingle bells and all?" A teasing light sparkled in his night-darkened eyes.

"Yes. Jingle bells and all." She smiled the admission, her gaze absently wandering over his features; the straight bridge of his nose, and the strong cut of his mouth.

"Look, Daddy. There's a covered bridge ahead!" Holly pulled her hand out from under the robe long enough to point out the houselike structure spanning a river.

"It certainly is."

"Are we going to go through it?" Holly wanted to know.

"I guess so," Tagg replied. "That's where the road goes—unless you want me to turn around and go back."

"No, I want to go across the bridge," she insisted.

As they drew closer, the white snow on the bridge's roof made its opening into the wooden tunnel appear even blacker. On the far side, the moonlight showed the way out.

"Why did they put covers on bridges?" Holly asked as she made a frowning study of the structure.

"These bridges were built a long time ago when most people traveled by horse and wagon. If it started raining or snowing, they could take shelter under the roofs of these bridges," Tagg explained, and slowed the mare to a walk as they entered the bridge tunnel.

Wind had whipped some snow and ice onto the reinforced woodplank floors. The horse's hooves echoed hollowly, disturbing an owl perched on a rafter. It hooted and swooped low to fly out into the night. Involuntarily, Leslie cringed and ducked, moving closer to Tagg before realizing it was just an owl. His hand tightened on hers, lifting her glance toward his shadowed face only inches away.

"I've also heard that during the old days when young men took their girl friends for courting rides in the buggy, these bridges made ideal lover's lanes," he murmured loud enough so Holly would think he was talking to her while he bent his head to claim Leslie's lips.

Initially his mouth felt cool against her lips, but it warmed up quickly, pressing on hers with a moist, demanding need. Her response was just as quick and just as hungry, trying to make up for the necessary shortness of the kiss.

There was the faintest sound as the contact was broken, seconds before they emerged from the covered bridge into the moonlight. His glance held hers for another second while his hand tucked hers more closely to him under the robe, their forearms resting together.

"Are we going to come back this way?" Holly asked.

"We could," Tagg admitted. "Why? Is that what you want to do?"

"No, but I thought it might be what you wanted to do." There was an impish little glint in her eyes when she looked at him.

"What makes you think that?" he asked with a trace of amusement in his voice.

"Oh, Daddy, I'm not a baby anymore," she

chided him in exasperation. "I heard you kiss Leslie. Besides, I know what a lover's lane is."

"I have an idea," Tagg said. "Why don't we sing?" He slid a sideways glance at Leslie. "Sorry, but if you can't beat 'em, join 'em. And you know what they say about little pitchers having big ears."

"You sing along, too, Leslie," Holly urged.

The choice of songs was a foregone conclusion. Under the circumstances, it had to be "Jingle Bells." This time Leslie did sing with them, her mellow mood making her overlook her usual prejudices about caroling.

And the singing didn't stop until their long, circling route brought them back to the house. The farmer was waiting in Tagg's driveway with a pickup truck and horsecar. When they turned in, the back door to her aunt's house opened and Patsy Evans stepped outside.

"You're invited over for cider and gingerbread!" she called.

While Tagg stayed to help the farmer load the horse and sleigh, Holly and Leslie crossed the yard to her aunt's house. After being outside in the cold so long, the kitchen felt toasty warm, the air fragrant with the spicy smell of freshly baked gingerbread.

"We had so much fun, Mrs. Evans!" Holly chattered nonstop while she peeled off her snow jacket and pants. "We sang and sang. And there was this covered bridge—"

"I think I sang so much I lost my voice," Leslie interrupted her, not certain how much the little girl would reveal. "My throat feels hoarse."

"It probably is, from the sound of it," her aunt declared, standing at the stove and ladling mulled cider into mugs for each of them. "There's a fire burning in the fireplace. Take these and go in there and get warmed up."

Leslie curved both hands around the mug of hot cider, shivering in delayed reaction to the cold now that she was getting warm. "Can you carry mine, too, Holly?" she asked, certain she'd spill it if she tried to carry it and use only one crutch.

"Sure." Holly took it from her and headed for the living room where the crackling fire beckoned.

The furniture was grouped around the fireplace. Leslie settled into the chair with the footstool in front of it and propped her leg on it. Just the sight of the fire was warming. Holly gave her one of the mugs, then sat on the floor, facing the burning logs. The hot apple cider was sweet with brown sugar and laced with cloves and cinnamon. Its spicy sweetness seemed to activate her tastebuds again.

The feeling had returned to her toes when Tagg finally joined them, bearing his own mug of mulled cider from the kitchen. He set it on the mantel and held his hands out to the flames, rubbing them briskly together.

"Cold?" Leslie asked him teasingly.

"Yes." His gaze challenged her. "Do you want to come warm me up?"

"Put another log on the fire instead," she countered.

"The other way would be faster," he insisted, amusement glinting in his eyes.

"Too bad I'm comfortable." She turned her head when she heard footsteps. Her aunt entered the living room, carrying a tray with steaming gingerbread squares, dollops of whipped cream melting over them. After they were passed around, conversation was forgotten until every last crumb had been consumed. Tagg washed his last bite down with a swig of mulled cider.

"That was delicious, Mrs. Evans," he stated.

"It was good," Patsy Evans agreed with him. "I thought you'd enjoy it after your sleigh ride." She started to gather up the dishes.

"I'll do that for you," Tagg insisted. "Leslie can show me where to put things."

Her aunt didn't argue with him as he stacked the

dishes onto the tray and waited for Leslie to lead the way into the kitchen. Once there, it was a simple matter to put the dirty dishes in the sink, cover the whipped cream with a plastic lid and set it in the refrigerator.

"Two shakes of a lamb's tail and we're done," Leslie announced, turning on her crutches and finding Tagg blocking her way.

"It didn't take very long, did it?" he curved an arm around her and gathered her body to his length. His hand moved caressingly over her cheek, down her neck, and tunneled under her hair. "Do you think they'll miss us? It sounds like Holly has your aunt occupied."

"Yes, it does." Her pulse accelerated under his touch, heat running through her veins. The sound of it hammering in her ears was about all she could hear and his face was blocking everything else out of her vision.

Her head was tipped backwards under the pressure of his moist kiss as his mouth rocked hungrily over her lips, eating at their softness. Then he was driving her lips apart and she was tasting the lingering spice on his tongue. Her breath was coming deep and fast, reacting to this intimate stimulation while a fiery inner glow seemed to melt her bones.

His attention gradually shifted to her cheekbone, the corner of her eye and the lobe of her ear. His nibbling and nuzzling sent off fresh waves of sensation, quivering over her nerve ends. She leaned more heavily against him, arching her spine to get closer to him still, yet her hands instinctively kept their grip on her crutches.

"Aunt Patsy is going to start wondering what's keeping us?" Leslie whispered against his skin.

"I'll bet she's already figured it out," he said thickly. His mouth searched out the corner of her lips, nuzzling it and letting their breath mingle. "Kiss me, Leslie."

She turned her lips into his mouth, a silent moan getting no farther than her throat. The shattering completeness of his kiss unleashed a greater need inside. Whirled away on this tide of intense longing, she forgot everything else and moved to put her arm around him.

Her crutches clattered to the floor with a resounding crash!

For a split second, it startled both of them, jarring them apart. Leslie realized instantly what she'd done and muttered impotently, "Damn this broken leg."

Running feet were already tearing toward the kitchen from the living room as Tagg bent down to retrieve the crutches. He was just handing them to her when Holly burst into the room.

"What happened?" she asked in wide-eyed alarm. "What was that racket?"

"Leslie dropped her crutches. It made a lot of noise, but that's all," Tagg assured her.

Her aunt appeared in the doorway behind Holly. "She didn't fall did she?"

"No," Leslie answered for herself. "The crutches just slipped out of my hands."

"Boy, it really scared me!" Holly declared, holding a hand to her throat. "I thought something terrible had happened."

"Nothing did," Tagg repeated. "You'd better get your things together. It's long past your bedtime."

"That's okay. I don't have school tomorrow. It's Saturday, remember?" she protested that the evening had to draw to a close so soon.

"Saturday or not, it's time you were in bed," he insisted, and crossed the kitchen to take his coat off the wall hook. "Thanks again for the cider and the gingerbread, Mrs. Evans."

"She said I could call her Aunt Patsy if I wanted," Holly informed him as she tried to get her arm into the other coat sleeve.

"Then tell her goodnight and thanks." Tagg helped her find the opening.

"Goodnight, Aunt Patsy, and thanks for everything." Now that the decision was made to leave, she wasn't taking any time over it. "Goodnight, Leslie."

"Goodnight." To Tagg, she added, "Thanks for asking me along tonight."

"Jingle Bells, Holly, and all." His mouth twitched with a brief smile before his glance shifted down to her lips, then he was reaching for the door and pushing Holly toward it. "Goodnight, Mrs. Evans."

After they had gone, her aunt walked over to the sink. "I'll wash up those dishes, Aunt Patsy," Leslie volunteered.

"There isn't even a good sinkful here. We'll do them with the breakfast dishes in the morning. I thought that you might have gotten your hands wet because you'd put them to soak. But I guess your crutches fell for some other reason." Her aunt didn't elaborate on what she thought the reason might be.

"Yes, I guess so."

"There's enough cider here for two more mugs." Her aunt checked the contents of the pan. "Shall we finish it?"

"Sure." Leslie moved to get the mugs.

"I've been thinking," her aunt began. "Maybe we

115

should ask Taggart and his daughter to come over Christmas Eve and have oyster stew with us."

"I think that would be a nice idea," Leslie agreed. "Maybe I could buy a little something for Holly— for a Christmas present."

"You could," her aunt nodded in an approving manner.

"I'll do it tomorrow," Leslie decided.

The next morning was as bright and clear as the previous night had been, and the temperature was almost as cold despite the golden sun shining down. Bundled up in her heavy jacket, gloves, and ski cap, Leslie was humming to herself as she did her three-legged walk down the driveway to the sidewalk.

"Where are you going, Leslie?" Holly came racing out of the house, her snow jacket unzipped and flopping open, and the hood barely staying on her head.

"I thought I'd walk into town. I need the exercise." She waited by the edge of the shoveled sidewalk while Holly came to a puffing stop beside her.

"Would you do me a favor?" Holly fumbled around, trying to get her hands into her pockets.

"What?" Leslie asked, discovering it was always wiser to ask first before agreeing.

"Will you mail this for me?" She finally found the crumpled envelope she had tucked in her pocket.

"Sure." Leslie took the envelope and slipped it into the coat pocket with her change purse.

"Thanks loads. Daddy doesn't know I'm outside, so I gotta go. Bye!" With a wave of her hand, Holly raced back for the house.

The village's small post office happened to be first along her route. Leslie paused by the drop box and reached in her pocket for the letter. When she checked to make sure it had a stamp, she noticed the address.

It read simply: "Santa Claus, North Pole."

"I can't believe I'm doing this," she muttered to herself and slipped the letter into the mail slot.

The village was small so naturally there were few stores and the selection of gifts for an almost-seven-year-old girl was limited. Leslie did find a couple of books that had been her favorites when she was about Holly's age, so she bought them and a hand-made bookmark. No doubt she'd get toys aplenty from Tagg—and Santa Claus.

With the wrapped parcel clamped between her arm and the crutch, she set off for her aunt's house again. A half a block away, she could hear Holly's giggling laughter. The bottom torso of a snowman was sitting in the middle of Tagg's front yard, but he was forgotten as Tagg and Holly hurled snowballs at each other.

Leslie watched them with a trace of sadness. Once she and her father had played like that—carefree and innocent. But that was long ago—before the arguments and bitter fights became so frequent. She hobbled forward, her head downcast.

A flying missile hit her shoulder with solid impact, splattering icy bits of snow onto her face. It knocked her off-balance. She heard Tagg shout as the tip of her crutch slid on a patch of ice. A startled cry came from her throat as she realized she was falling.

Out of instinct, she twisted her body to shield her broken limb and attempt to aim herself at the deep snow piled beside the walk. She landed hard, the packed snow making a crunching sound beneath. For the first few seconds, she was too shocked to move while her mind made a swift mental check to see if she was hurt. Nothing seemed to be damaged but her pride. She pushed a hand into the snow to lever herself upright.

Tagg came to a skidding stop beside her spraying snow in her face again. He dropped to one knee, bending over her. "Leslie, are you all right? I swear I didn't see you when I threw that snowball."

"I think I'm all right," she murmured shakily.

"Better let me help you up," he said and began to tunnel an arm under her side to lift her.

The shock of the fall had worn off, leaving a small, but vengeful anger in its place. Her gloved fingers dug into the snow, snatching up a handful which she tossed in his face as she turned as if to aid him in lifting her.

His head jerked backwards as he sputtered and wiped at the snow that clung to his eyelashes and mouth. His look was first filled with surprise, then retaliatory amusement.

Off to the side, Holly laughed and jumped up and down. "She got you, Daddy!"

"You little witch," Tagg growled at Leslie, but his humor-riddled tone took any menace from his voice.

"You deserved that," she retorted and finished the turn so she could sit up and begin brushing the snow off her.

Out of the corner of her eye, Leslie saw Tagg reach down and scoop up a handful of snow. It triggered a warning of his intentions. With upraised arms, Leslie tried to shield herself from the expected snowball, but Tagg caught at her hand instead. He paid no attention to her laughter-laced outcry of protest as she struggled with him, warding off the hand with the snow. His strength and pressing weight was forcing her backward.

"Watch my leg!" she warned him with a squeal and tried to dodge the hand attempting to rub the snow in her face.

Breathless laughter was claiming both of them as they tumbled onto the snowbank, Tagg taking care to stay away from her legs. When he couldn't reach her face, he pushed the handful of snow down her neck. Leslie shrieked at the sudden cold against her skin and tried to do the same to him.

But he caught her wrist. A second later, her arms were pinned against the snow and the upper part of his body was lying across her to hold her down. Out of breath and laughing, Leslie stopped struggling and glanced at the male face above her. His mouth was parted in a panting smile of triumph.

"Give up?" Tagg asked, breathing hard from the short tussle in the cold, morning air.

"Yes." Her admission of defeat came out on a puffing breath.

His hold on her forearms relaxed, but it wasn't taken away. In the twinkling of an eye, the playful atmosphere changed and became charged with an elemental tension. Her breaths lengthened out under the darkening glitter of his gaze while her swiftly racing pulse took on a disturbed beat.

An awareness ran through both of them at the intimate positions of their prone bodies. The searching probe of his gaze moved over her face and became diverted by her parted lips. More of his weight began to settle onto her as Tagg began to slowly lower his head.

"Aren't you going to let her up, Daddy?" Holly's puzzled question short-circuited the volatile currents running between them.

Turning his head to the side, Tagg dragged in a deep breath and shifted his hold to clasp her arms. As he straightened backward, he pulled Leslie with him, sitting her up. The wryness in his blue eyes showed an amused regret when he met Leslie's sparkling glance.

"I swear, Holly—" his gaze slid to his daughter, "—Cupid would never choose you for an accomplice."

Holly frowned at him. "What's an accomplice?"

"Get Leslie's crutches for her." Tagg ignored her question.

When his feet were solidly under him, he spanned her waist with his hands and lifted her up to stand precariously balanced on one foot, her fingers gripping the sleeve of his coat for support. Holly retrieved the crutches and dragged them over to Leslie. Tagg brushed at the snow sticking to her coat, slapping off the worst of it.

"Are you all right?" His warm and lazy glance moved over the subdued radiance in her eyes.

"Yes." She nodded briefly, a small smile showing.

There was a clump of snow on the collar of her coat. Tagg reached over and brushed it off, then let the gloved tips of his fingers touch her neck before lifting strands of golden tan hair outside her collar. Despite the coldness of his gloves, she was warmed by the light, tingling caress.

"I'd better walk you to the house so you don't get knocked off your feet again," he said.

Leslie took one step, then remembered. "I had a package." She looked around for it and spied the present sticking out of a snowdrift.

"I'll get it for you." Holly noticed it at the same instant.

At the sight of the Christmas-wrapped present, Tagg quirked an eyebrow at her. "What's this?" he murmured dryly. "I thought you didn't go in for last minute Christmas shopping."

"There's an exception to every rule," she retorted and started to take the package from Holly, relieved to notice the paper hadn't been torn.

"Better let me carry it." Tagg took it from his daughter, and gestured for Leslie to go ahead of him. "I'll catch you if you fall."

"Promises from the man who knocked me down," Leslie mocked.

"Ah, but I picked you back up again and brushed you off," Tagg reminded her with a twinkling glance as they started up the driveway toward the house.

Holly split away from them. "I'm going to work on our snowman."

"Don't be throwing any snowballs," Tagg warned with a faint smile and let his gaze follow his young daughter as she took off for their front yard where the partially constructed snowman waited.

"Do you have any plans for Christmas Eve?" Leslie asked, then explained the reason for the question. "Aunt Patsy and I would like you and Holly to come over and have oyster stew with us."

"We accept."

She remembered something else. "Oh, would you tell Holly that I mailed her letter to Santa Claus?"

A surprised frown flickered across his features. "When?"

"This morning. She saw me leaving and ran out to give it to me," Leslie explained. "Why?"

"We already mailed one letter to him last week." His glance strayed briefly to his daughter, a certain puzzled certainty in his expression; then Tagg shrugged it away. "I guess she decided to put in a second request for a dog."

"Is Santa going to bring her one?" A smile twitched at her mouth.

"Santa is still looking," he answered dryly.

Taking the lead up the steps, Tagg held the doors open for her and followed her into the kitchen with the gift-wrapped package. Her aunt was standing by the wall phone, the receiver to her ear. She half-turned when she heard them enter.

"My niece just walked in," she said to the party on the line. "I'll ask her and call you later to let you know. Goodbye."

"Ask me what?" Leslie inquired when her aunt hung up the phone.

"Hello, Taggart," she greeted him first before answering Leslie's question. "That was Maude Freer on the phone, a dear friend of mine who lost her husband this fall. She called to ask me to come have dinner with her Thursday night. When I explained you were visiting me, she asked you to come with me. Naturally you can stay here if you'd rather."

"Why don't you have dinner with Holly and me that night?" Tagg suggested.

"I'd like that," Leslie accepted his invitation, then glanced at her aunt. "You don't mind, do you?"

"Of course not. If I was your age, I certainly wouldn't want to spend an evening in the company of two widowed ladies when I could be with a good-looking man instead."

"Why, thank you, Mrs. Evans." Tagg inclined his head at the implied compliment, the corners of his mouth deepening with a suppressed smile.

"Then it's all settled. I'll call Maude back and let her know," Patsy Evans stated decisively.

Tagg set her package on the counter and reached for the doorknob to leave. "Thursday night, around six?"

"That's fine." Leslie nodded her agreement.

# CHAPTER

# 7

A HARD CRUST had formed on the old snow. It crunched under her crutches like the breaking of ice, leaving clear-cut holes in the snow. New snowflakes swirled all around Leslie as she took a shortcut across the driveway and the Williams's front yard to the door. It was like being inside the glass dome of a winter scene after someone had shaken it.

The front porch light was on, throwing its light into the early evening darkness to show Leslie the way to the steps. The snow had begun falling as gentle flurries, but the flakes were coming down in earnest now. She clumped up the steps and across the wooden porch floor to the front door, punching the bell.

The muted echo of the doorbell had barely faded when Holly yanked the door open to admit her. Leslie swung across the threshold on her crutches and paused inside the door to lean her weight on them. The cold air had left her slightly out of breath. She smiled at Tagg when he came to greet her.

"I was hoping you'd come early," Holly declared. "We've almost got dinner ready, but I wanted to show you all the presents under the tree."

"Give Leslie a chance to take her coat off before you drag her off," Tagg said with an indulgent smile and moved forward to help her out of it.

"It's really coming down out there." Leslie loosened the wool scarf around her neck. White crystalline flakes were quickly melting to leave diamond drops sparkling in her tawny hair. "I hope it doesn't get too bad before Aunt Patsy leaves to come home."

"She's lived in Vermont most of her life. She knows how to drive in this kind of weather, so I wouldn't worry about her having any difficulty," Tagg replied, helping to slip her arm out of one coat sleeve, then the other.

When Tagg moved away to hang up her coat in the front closet, Leslie brushed at the melting snow on her clothes. Her calf-length skirt of camel tan concealed most of the plaster cast on her left leg. The rest of it was covered by a brown sock, the same shade as the tall, heeled boot she wore on her right foot. Adorning the plain white turtleneck sweater she was wearing, there was a large, gold medallion necklace in the design of an Aztec sun. She paused to adjust the clasp behind her neck.

Holly tugged at her arm, laughing up at her. "Leslie, Daddy's standing under the mistletoe."

When she lifted her head, she saw Tagg looking up at the ribboned sprig of mistletoe above him. "Sure enough. It's up there," he declared, bringing his glinting gaze down level with hers. "Now, I wonder how that happened." The faint curve of his mouth challenged her to carry out the tradition.

"I wonder, too," Leslie mocked, aware of Holly's silent urging.

It was only a few swinging strides to where he was standing. Leslie crossed the space and pushed on the crutches to raise herself on tiptoe while he tilted his head down. This mistletoe kiss wasn't as brief as the first one had been, their lips moving together in a warmly ardent greeting after being so long apart.

An involuntary sigh trembled through her when she drew away, the raw sweetness of the controlled exchange making her want to get rid of the bonds of propriety. Tagg held her gaze for a long moment, his nostrils distended as if drinking in the perfumed fragrance of her and memorizing it. Then his attention swung reluctantly to his daughter as if needing to remind himself of her presence.

"You can show Leslie all the presents now while I take the food to the table," he said.

"Come over here, Leslie." Holly waved her toward the lighted tree in the living room.

Leslie was slow to follow the little girl. Her gaze traveled after Tagg as he cut through the dining room toward the kitchen. Slim-fitting black slacks accented his narrow-hipped and long-legged build and the heavily ribbed smoke blue sweater hinted at the muscular strength of his chest and shoulders. As the other girls in the office would say, he was "some hunk of man" with his hair gleaming blue-black in the interior light.

"Do you see this one, Leslie?" Holly's voice demanded her attention, breaking into her thoughts. "It's so heavy I can't pick it up. And it's got my name on it, too."

"What do you suppose is in it?" Leslie asked the expected question.

"I don't know, and Daddy won't give me any clues," Holly grimaced in mild exasperation. "See this one."

After Leslie had dutifully looked at the packages under the tree, Holly led her into the dining room. "You sit here." She pulled out a chair for her as Tagg arrived with the platter of roast beef. All the rest of the food was already on the table.

"It smells delicious," Leslie declared, taking her seat.

"It should. We've been slaving in the kitchen all afternoon, haven't we, Holly?" Tagg asked his daughter for confirmation of his mocking remark.

"We've got pumpkin pie for dessert," she informed Leslie. "And I helped make it. I helped Daddy cook everything." After thinking about that, Holly qualified her expansive statement. "Well, almost everything."

Leslie wasn't sure whether it was the food or the company, but she couldn't remember the last time she had enjoyed a meal so much. Even clearing the table and washing the dirty dishes afterward was kinda fun with all three of them pitching in to do their share. Leslie washed, Tagg dried, and Holly put them away.

Then it was hot chocolate in the living room with the crackle of logs burning in the fireplace. It wasn't long until the hypnotic flames had weaved a silent spell on all of them. Leslie didn't notice the quiet until it was broken by the slap of Tagg's hand on Holly's leg. The two of them were seated on the couch while Leslie occupied the matching chair and ottoman.

"School tomorrow, little lady," Tagg stated lazily. "It's time for you to get to bed."

If Holly intended to protest, she thought better of it when she was overtaken by a sleepy yawn. "Okay." She pushed off the sofa and walked over to kiss him goodnight. "Can Leslie come up and tuck me in?"

The request appeared to catch him off guard, then he threw a questing look at Leslie. "She might not want to climb the stairs." He offered her an excuse if she wanted to use it, but she was oddly touched by Holly's request.

"I think me and my trusty crutches can manage them," she assured Holly. "You call me when you're ready."

"Okay." She headed for the maplewood staircase at a running walk and went up the steps at the same pace.

"I hope you don't mind," Tagg said. "It's probably a novelty to have a woman tuck her into bed."

"It'll be a novelty for me, too," Leslie replied and listened to the muffled noises overhead.

"More cocoa?" he asked.

"No thanks." She shook her head.

"I'll just take these mugs out to the kitchen." He rolled to his feet and collected the empty cocoa cups.

Tagg was just returning to the living room when Holly called down, "I'm ready!"

"I'll be back." Leslie smiled at Tagg and headed for the stairs.

The steps were nice and wide, giving her plenty of room to maneuver her crutches. At the head of the stairs, a door was standing open to a lighted room. Holly was sitting cross-legged on the single bed with the covers turned back, waiting for Leslie. She came into the room, not too sure what was expected from her.

"You have a nice room, Holly."

Blue-flowered wallpaper covered the walls with matching light blue curtains and bedspread, as well as a skirted vanity table painted white like the rest of the woodwork. A few dolls and some of her toys were arranged neatly on white shelves. The bedside lamp had a frilly white shade.

"I'm glad you came up to tuck me in," Holly stated when Leslie lowered herself to sit on the edge of the bed.

"So am I." She lifted the covers so Holly could slide her legs under them.

"You like my daddy, don't you?" Holly folded her hands behind her head, watching Leslie with her round, innocent blue eyes. Long black hair spilled across the pillow case.

"Yes, I do," Leslie admitted.

"He likes you, too. And I'm glad," she stated.

"Because I like you a lot. I wish you lived here all the time instead of just staying here over the holidays."

"New York isn't that far away. I can come here to visit again," Leslie reminded her. "Because I like you a lot, too."

A happy smile split Holly's face. She pulled her arms down and snuggled under the covers. "Good night, Leslie."

"Goodnight, Holly." It suddenly seemed perfectly natural to bend over and kiss the girl's soft cheek. When she was standing, Leslie looked down at the child. "Shall I leave a light on?"

"No. I'm not afraid of the dark," Holly assured her.

She switched off the lamp and moved toward the lighted stairwell. The telephone rang as she started down the steps. She heard Tagg answer it, but her thoughts were on Holly so she didn't listen to his side of the conversation.

All the lights in the living room had been turned off except for the winking Christmas tree lights and the flickering glow from the fireplace. The room's dimness made for an intimate atmosphere. Leslie paused beside the ottoman, turning when she heard Tagg coming.

"That was your aunt on the phone," he informed her. "She decided the roads were too icy so she's going to stay the night with her friend rather than drive home."

"Is it getting worse outside?" Leslie glanced toward the steamed-over window but it was impossible to see out.

"It's coming down pretty thick," he admitted. "Your aunt said the weatherman on the radio is predicting six to ten inches by morning."

She lowered herself onto the ottoman so she could be closer to the fire. "As the song says, 'Let it snow.' "

"I agree." Tagg stretched out his length on the floor in front of her, propped on one elbow and looking into the leaping flames curling up from the charred white logs edged with red.

"What's with the lights?" Leslie asked with a faint smile, leaning forward to rest her arms on her knee. "Conserving energy?"

"I could have turned the lights down low, but I turned them off," he admitted, his mouth quirking on one side. He turned the upper half of his body toward her and held out his arm. "How else could I create the right mood to suggest you come down here with me?"

Accepting the invitation and his assistance, Leslie lay down on the warm carpet beside him with her head pillowed on his arm. He turned onto his side, facing her, and kissed at her lips, then drew back.

"Alone at last," he murmured.

"It's always possible Holly might decide she wants a drink of water," Leslie murmured to tease him.

"If she does, I'll drown her," Tagg growled the mock threat.

"No, you won't," she laughed softly.

"Don't be too sure," he warned. "I've been wanting to be alone with you for a long time."

When he lowered his mouth onto hers, its raw passion seemed to prove his patience had reached its limits. Her arms wound around him holding on while her senses were shaken by the answering rush of heat. With moist and mobile force, he kissed her lips apart and tasted the fullness of her response opening up to him. She was gathered close against him, her breasts feeling the solidness of his chest through the knitted material of her sweater.

For heated moments, the exchange continued while the blood pounded through her veins. Her breath was coming heavy and fast when Tagg grazed her cheek with kisses and pushed the hair away from her ear to take nibbling lovebites at the lobe. The high, rolled collar of her turtleneck sweater impeded his attempt to explore the sensitive cords in her throat and neck.

"Do you know what the trouble with winter is?" His warm breath spilled over her skin as his lips formed the words against her cheek.

"What?" she whispered, thinking it was a silly question at this particular time.

"People wear too many clothes, especially women," Tagg said quickly. Aware of his hand getting tangled in the knit folds of her loose sweater, Leslie laughed, but it was a breathless, barely audible sound. "You can never be sure what's under them until you take them off."

She felt his hand pushing up the hem of her sweater and the tightness in her throat began to spread upward, too. "A person could catch cold without them, so maybe it's wise."

"Wise men never fall in love." He began to sit up, bringing her with him.

For a second, she watched him take hold of the bottom of his smoke blue sweater to remove it. Then she pulled hers over her head, shaking her hair free and laying the sweater on the ottoman. When she turned back to Tagg, he was wearing a bemused look as he stared at her flesh-colored cotton camisole.

"What's this?" he asked, touching a shoulder strap with the end of his finger.

"A camisole."

"What happened to lacy brassieres with convenient hooks?" he complained as he searched for the camisole's hem and found it, lifting the loose undergarment over her head, and tossing it onto the ottoman.

Tagg gave her no time to become self-conscious with her partial nudity or his own. His arms were immediately around her and gently lowering her to the floor once again. The heat of his bare flesh was under her hands, the iron-solid muscles rippling with easy strength.

Their kisses became longer and hungrier while his roaming hands excited her with their touch. She was fast losing control over what she was doing. His teeth nibbled sensually at a white shoulder, sending quivers all through her nerve ends. Her fingers combed into the virile thickness of his hair as his mouth trailed up the slope of her breast to reach its hard peak. She felt herself slipping.

This was not turning out to be a simple necking and petting spree. It was becoming the preliminary to something infinitely more intimate. All the achings and longings of her flesh were seeking it but Leslie wasn't sure if she was ready.

Abruptly she pulled away from him and sat up, breathing in deeply in her fight for a sanity beyond lust. "You're going too fast for me," she stated unevenly and pushed at her hair.

His hand slid to the front of her waist. "You're

going too slow for me," Tagg countered, and pressed his lips to the small of her back.

An exquisite shudder of raw pleasure ran through her, closing her eyes. "I can't think clearly." Especially now when his mouth was working its way up her spine. "And I don't like decisions forced on me if I'm not ready to make them. And I'm not ready to make this one." She felt him lifting the hair away from the nape of her neck and knew she had to stop his progress. Leslie half-turned and reached for her clothes. "It's time I went home."

His hand took the weight of her breast and pulled her back to him. Her sensitized skin felt the heat and solidness of his hair-roughened chest. She curled her fingers into her sweater and camisole, clutching them to her taut stomach.

"Honey, it's cold outside," Tagg murmured in a reasoning and persuasive tone. "Listen to that wind."

Above the thundering of her racing heart, Leslie could hear the muffled howl of the north wind and realized the storm had intensified. "It's just going to get worse out there. I might as well leave now." But her voice trailed off on a weakening note as he nuzzled at the erotic pleasure point at the base of her neck.

"Why go out in the storm when you can stay the night here?" Tagg asked. "With me."

"But that's just it," she protested and this time made a determined effort to escape both his touch and his kisses by twisting sideways and scooting backward out of his hold. "I don't know if it's what I want." That wasn't precisely true and Leslie shook her head in agitation. "It is what I want, but I'm not sure why."

"Do you have to analyze it?" he challenged mildly, but made no attempt to physically bring her back into his arms.

"Yes," she answered with a trace of impatience. "I don't know if I'm feeling this way because I'm lonely and I want to be held by someone—whether I've merely become sexually aroused—or if I feel obligated to let you make love to me because I've willingly gone this far already and you expect me to go the rest of the way. I just don't know."

She tugged the camisole over her head and followed it with the sweater, not even bothering to check front from back. As she adjusted the sweater around her waist, Leslie finally looked at him. Tagg sat there, braced on one arm, the firelight bathing his wide shoulders and the ruffled mat of hair on his naked chest, the corded muscles of his flat stomach standing out tautly. But the flickering light cast shadows on his tanned and angular features, making their expression unreadable.

His hand reached out to her and Leslie managed

not to shy away from it. He lifted her sand-colored hair outside of the high collar of her turtleneck and let it lay about her shoulders.

"In all the reasons you mentioned, you left out an important one," Tagg said quietly and shifted his position to rest both hands on her shoulders near the base of her neck. "Maybe you love me. Maybe I want you to stay because I love you."

"It's a possibility," she whispered tightly, and felt pulled into the deep blue of his eyes.

"Leslie." His head moved slightly from side to side in faint negative movement. "It's more than a possibility that I love you."

A tremor vibrated through her at his low, charged statement. It was more than possible she loved him but there were too many purely physical sensations that were controlling her.

"Tagg, I'm not sure." It was imperative that there be no doubt in her mind. To her, love meant a lifetime commitment. It was too easy to be mistaken about emotions. How many people married someone they felt they loved only to discover their mistake in divorce courts? That wasn't going to happen to her.

Tagg let her go, reaching for his sweater. "Then I'll take you to your aunt's." His voice sounded gruff.

She guessed that she had inadvertently hurt him, but guilt was not sufficient reason to say something she wasn't absolutely sure about. She looked around for her crutches.

"Where are my crutches?" She didn't see them by the ottoman where she thought she had put them.

"I hid them," Tagg said dryly and reached under the coffee table to pull them out. "I said to myself, 'How far could a classy lady with a broken leg get without her crutches?' And I answered myself that she wouldn't get away from me if I didn't want to let her go."

"That's terrible to take advantage like that," Leslie accused.

Anger flashed in his suddenly cold eyes. "I was only joking. I put them there so they'd be out of the way," he snapped.

"Oh." It was a small sound, tinged with guilt that she had been so quick to believe he might do that. "I'm sorry."

"You should be," he muttered and rolled to his feet, walking to the end table by the sofa to snap on the lamp.

There was a click, but no light came on. Leslie became instantly aware the only light in the room came from the fireplace.

"The tree lights are out," she told Tagg.

He moved toward the wall, his figure becoming

partially obscured by the shadows. She heard the click of a switch, but the darkness remained.

"Stay there," he ordered. "I'm going to get a flashlight and check the fuse box."

Scooting along the carpet, dragging her leg with its cast, Leslie moved closer to the fire as the sound of his footsteps retreated toward the rear portion of the house. She stirred the glowing red embers with the brass poker. Flames shot up to throw more light into the room. Shadows eerily danced along the wall.

A long time seemed to pass before she saw a flashlight beam throwing a pool of moving light onto the floor and heard his footsteps behind it.

"The storm must have snapped a wire somewhere. There's no electricity and no lights showing anywhere outside," he stated grimly.

Switching off the flashlight to conserve the batteries, Tagg walked over and added another log to the fire. Sparks flew, lighting up his face. It took a minute for Leslie to realize he meant the power was out in her aunt's house as well.

"Like it or not—" his glance swung to her, —you're going to have to spend the night here. Without electricity, there isn't any heat, here or at your aunt's house."

"She uses oil to heat her house," Leslie corrected him.

"Yes, but it takes electricity to operate the blower motor and the thermostat controls," Tagg stated. "We'll have to rely on the fireplace."

"I'm going home." She levered herself up using the arm of the chair until she could get her crutches under her. "With no heat over there, her water pipes will freeze and break."

Tagg moved to block her way. "Leslie, I don't want you spending the night over there by yourself." He raked a hand through his hair in a gesture of agitated exasperation. "Listen, I don't want to come on like a heavy-handed male who is determined to have things his way. But—dammit! I'm not going to spend the night here, worrying about you over there with that broken leg—wondering whether you're warm enough—or if you've fallen. Whether you can take care of yourself or not, I'd worry."

"But the water pipes—" She was swayed by his genuine concern and the phrasing of his appeal— not claiming that he was stronger, but simply in a better position to cope.

"I'll go over there myself and turn the faucets on," he promised. "For my own peace of mind, will you please spend the night here? I can't leave Holly here by herself—and it would be foolish for all three of us to go traipsing over there."

"I'll stay," Leslie agreed.

His mouth curved in a faintly relieved smile. "Okay, first things, first. I'll go upstairs and bring Holly down. All three of us will have to sleep in front of the fireplace tonight."

"We should close off the living room, too, so we can keep all the warmth we can confined in here," Leslie suggested.

"Good idea." He looked at her with approval. "I can hang a blanket across the opening. We should have enough extra blankets to spare for that." He started for the stairs.

While he was gone, Leslie went over to the windows to draw the drapes and close out any drafts. She returned to the fireplace to wait.

Holly was certain it was an adventure as exciting as camping out when Tagg carried her down the stairs, wrapped up in her bed blankets. She wanted to get the candles from the kitchen so they could have lights, but Leslie convinced her there was more than enough light to see by from the fireplace and the candles should be saved for an emergency.

After Tagg brought down an armload of blankets, he nailed one of them across the living room archway. It immediately seemed warmer in the room. She and Holly spread the rest of the blankets on the floor in front of the fireplace to make one large bed.

"Are we going to have to cook breakfast in the

fireplace, too?" Holly asked, all wide-eyed at the idea.

"Hopefully the electricity will be back on when we wake up in the morning," Leslie punctured that thought. "Climb under the blankets."

"I bet we won't have school tomorrow." Now that she was awake, Holly wasn't interested in going back to sleep and missing any more excitement. "It's snowing like everything outside, isn't it, Daddy?" She looked around, but he had disappeared behind the blanket curtain. "Where's Daddy? Do you suppose something happened to him?"

"No—"

The blanket lifted as Tagg stepped into the living room, all bundled up in his coat and ski hat. "I'm going over to your aunt's," he told Leslie. "Both of you get under those blankets. If you get chilled, it isn't going to be so easy to get warm again."

Following his advice, Leslie slipped under the blankets with Holly, letting the girl lie close to the fire. After Tagg had left, Holly chattered away, not expecting lengthy responses from Leslie. Eventually the dancing flames and the warmth of the blankets made the pauses between Holly's comments longer and longer.

In the quiet, Leslie listened to the creaking of the house and the wind prowling outside, occasionally rattling the window panes. With the reassuring crackle of the fire's warmth close by, she thought about Tagg, wondering whether he was still at her aunt's or making his way back through the snowstorm. It seemed he had been gone an awfully long time.

The front door opened, and the curtain-blanket billowed with the sudden sweep of cold air. Relief shivered through her when she heard the door being pushed shut and the stamp of his feet. Holly stirred sleepily beside her.

"What's that?" she murmured.

"Sssh. It's just your daddy," Leslie whispered.

Cold, cold air swirled into the room when the blanket was lifted aside and Tagg walked in, shuddering and rubbing his arms to get the circulation going. His glance ran first to Leslie, an attempt at a smile lifting his mouth, then to his sleeping daughter. Moving silently, he went to the fireplace and crouched in front of it.

"Is everything all right?" Leslie whispered.

He gave her an affirmative nod and stirred up the coals before adding another log to the fire. But he continued to shiver.

"You'd better get under the blankets," she advised.

When he slipped under the covers beside her, his clothes felt ice-cold. Leslie put her arms around him

146

and cradled his head on her shoulder, absorbing the tremors shivering through him. His hair and skin were cold. As his body began stealing her heat, she felt the penetrating chill.

"I'm making you cold," Tagg realized.

"It doesn't matter. We'll both be warm soon," she murmured, and held him more tightly.

In time, her statement came true. By then, all three of them were sleeping in the glow of the fireplace.

# CHAPTER

8

THE RUMBLE OF the snowplow wakened Leslie to the muted light behind the drapes drawn across the windows. She blinked sleepily in the semidarkness and tried to move, but she was sandwiched between two warm bodies.

Holly was curled tightly up against her, sleeping in the crook of her arm while Tagg's hugging length pressed itself to her other side. He was turned on his side, toward her with one leg lying across hers and a hand rested familiarly on her breast. His dark head was very close to hers on the pillow, his warm breath stirring the hair near her ear.

It was impossible to move without waking one or both of them, so Leslie subsided, resigning herself to the discomfort of the hard floor a little longer. She breathed in the air's chill and glanced sideways at the fireplace. The logs had burned down to chunks of white ash, the fire appearing to be out. But it was warm and cozy under the layers of blankets.

The hand on her breast moved, his fingers flexing and feeling in an intimately caressing manner. Leslie shifted slightly on the pillow trying to see if Tagg was awake. Her arm was pinned to her side by the pressing length of his body, so solid and warm. Thick and spiky male lashes lay together, leading Leslie to believe he still slept.

Then Tagg stirred, snuggling deeper into the pillow while his hand spread possessively over her breast. "What a wonderful way to wake up in the morning," he murmured without opening his eyes. "This is how it's supposed to be."

The lazy contentment in his voice sent a warm feeling of pleasure stealing through her. Leslie turned her head a little more in his direction, the corners of her mouth curving up. Through the screening veil of her lashes, she studied the easy strength in his masculine features, the shadowy growth of a night's beard on the teak brown skin stretched from cheekbone to jaw, and the attractive grooves that gentled his mouth. His eyes slowly opened, their dark centers ringed by a pale blue.

"I think the fire went out," Leslie whispered.

There was a lazy twitch of his mouth in amusement. "Do you want to bet on it?" Tagg murmured, putting another meaning into her words.

Her pulse gave a little leap of anticipation as he moved, without apparent effort, to lean slightly over her and lower his mouth onto her lips, moving over them in a mobile fashion.

It was a persuasive and pervasive kiss, warm with the fire of latent passion that started a curling heat spreading through Leslie. Even the faint scrape of the stubble on his chin seemed to be pleasantly rough, like the dry lick of a cat's tongue.

Tagg broke off the kiss with a degree of suddenness and turned his head to glance at his daughter nestled against Leslie's side. "You are supposed to be asleep," he accused with mock gruffness.

"I was pretending." Her voice bubbled with contained laughter. "I heard you and Leslie whispering and it woke me up."

His look was drolly resigned as his gaze slid to Leslie. "We should have shouted. She probably would have slept through that." Shifting his weight away from them, Tagg pushed aside the covers to get up. "I'll get the fire going again—the one in the fireplace," he added with a quirking smile.

"There won't be any school today, will there?"

Holly asked, rolling onto her side and off Leslie's arm to watch her father poke at the slumbering embers before adding more firewood.

"We'll have to turn the radio on and find out." Tagg didn't hazard a guess.

When the logs started smoking, Tagg moved away from the hearth and crossed to the windows to pull the drapes. Sunlight burst into the room. Leslie flinched and turned her head away from the blinding brightness until her eyes adjusted to it.

"It looks like a beautiful day outside. Cold but beautiful," he stated, and rubbed his hands together to ward off the room's coolness. "I sure could go for some coffee."

"What are we going to have for breakfast? I'm hungry," Holly declared.

"I guess it will have to be cereal and milk," he shrugged.

"Can't we toast some bread over the fire?" His daughter was determined to do some kind of cooking over the open flames.

"You can toast some bread," Tagg consented. "The main road has been plowed, so it shouldn't be long before the power is restored. I'll let you two ladies use the bathroom first while I rustle together some breakfast."

"Brrr. I don't want to leave the blankets," Holly

declared with an exaggerated shiver. "Do you, Leslie?"

"No, but we're going to have to sooner or later," she reasoned.

"Both of you, rise and shine." Tagg walked over and picked up the ends of the blankets. Holly squealed and grabbed to hold onto them, but he yanked them off, forcing them both to get up whether they wanted to or not.

Holly went scampering off to lead the way to the downstairs bathroom, shivering and carrying on with a child's theatrics, while Leslie followed at a necessarily slower pace. After sleeping in her clothes, her skirt especially was badly wrinkled. No amount of smoothing could rid the tan material of all its creases.

It was too cold for either Holly or Leslie to spend much time in the bathroom, making do with a quick, invigorating wash and a fast comb through their hair. When they returned to the partitioned-off living room, a cereal box and a pitcher of milk were sitting on the coffee table. Tagg entered the room shortly after they arrived, bringing a loaf of bread, a long-handled fork and a jar of strawberry preserves.

"You're in luck, Holly," he said. "I just heard on the radio there won't be any classes at school today."

"Yippee!" she shouted.

"Which means," Tagg continued, "you can help me shovel the sidewalks."

Holly groaned and ran to the window to see how much snow had accumulated in the night. But she was sidetracked by the discovery, "The treelights are on!"

With the power restored, it didn't take long for the central furnace to rid the house of its chill. Tagg made coffee, but Holly insisted they use the fire to toast their bread instead of the electric toaster. By the time they finished breakfast and a second cup of coffee, it was warm enough in the house for Tagg to take down the blanket across the living room opening.

"Let's get these blankets folded up, Holly," Leslie suggested and reached for the top one.

"We can do it later," Holly protested.

"I have to go home later," she reminded her, "and make sure everything is all right at Aunt Patsy's house."

"You'd better let me shovel a path over there first," Tagg said. "There's no sense trying to wade through all that snow on those crutches."

While he went outside to clear the walks, Leslie enlisted Holly's aid to pick up the front room and wash their breakfast dishes. When the housework was done, she checked his progress. There was a pathway through the snow nearly to her aunt's side door.

Anxious to make certain the blackout had not created any broken water pipes at her aunt's house, Leslie donned her heavy coat and wool scarf. Holly bundled up, too, to join her.

"Careful. It's slick!" Tagg called the warning to them when they emerged from the house.

As Leslie reached the edge of the driveway, she heard a car slowing down to turn in. It was her aunt returning home. She waited until the car was driven past her to the rear garage before she crossed to the side door. Tagg leaned on the snow shovel, his tanned complexion turned ruddy by the invigorating cold.

Holly went galloping through the snow to greet Patsy Evans as she waded toward the door. "We don't have any school today because of the snow," Holly informed her. "Did the electricity go out where you were? Ours was out all night."

"It was out at my friend's house, too," she replied.

"I came over last night and turned on the water in your sinks so the pipes wouldn't freeze," Tagg informed her. "Leslie spent the night at our place."

"That's a relief," her aunt stated. "I was concerned about her being in the house alone with no heat."

"We slept on the floor in front of the fireplace last night," Holly explained eagerly. "We had to huddle together under the blankets to keep warm. It was fun."

"I'm sure it was," Patsy agreed dryly.

"Did you have any trouble getting home this morning?" Leslie asked.

"It was a bit tricky getting out of Maude's driveway, but she lives on the main road so it had already been plowed. I had no trouble at all once I was on the road," she insisted. "But it certainly was nasty last night."

"Daddy—" Holly looked suddenly anxious, "will they cancel our Christmas program at church Sunday night because of this snow?"

"It won't be cancelled," Tagg assured her. "Not unless it snows again."

"Oh, good," Holly declared with very definite relief, and glanced up at the white-haired woman bundled up like an Eskimo in her fur-lined parka. "Are you coming to see our Christmas program?"

A pleased look brightened her expression, despite the chilling cold. "How nice of you to ask, Holly. I think Leslie and I would enjoy coming to watch your play." She glanced at her niece for confirmation.

"Aren't you coming?" Holly looked at her as if it had been a foregone conclusion that she would attend.

"Sure, we'll both come," Leslie promised, knowing how important it had been when she was a child to have people she knew in the audience at school or social functions.

"There's no need to take two cars," Tagg inserted. "All of us can go in our station wagon."

"That's very sensible," Patsy Evans agreed with his proposal. "What time shall we be ready?"

"The program starts at six-thirty, but Holly needs to be at the church early so why don't we leave at six?" Tagg suggested.

"We'll come over before six," she nodded her approval then glanced at Leslie with a no-nonsense briskness. "I don't know why we're standing out here in the cold when we can be inside. Thank you for looking after things, Taggart."

"It was nothing." He shrugged away her thanks and stepped to the side so they could get to the door. "Come on, Holly. Go get your shovel so we can get these walks cleared."

A check of the house showed a night of below-freezing temperatures had not resulted in any damage. Yet Leslie knew that events during the storm had resulted in changes within herself. As much as she was physically and emotionally attracted to Tagg, the feelings were also plagued by a vague apprehension. In the beginning it had been all right to take things as they came, but it was time she gave some serious thought about where their relationship was leading while there was still time to change its direction.

On Sunday evening, Leslie sat in the church pew between Tagg and her aunt, watching the Christmas story being acted out by the church's Sunday School class. Her view of Holly in a white and woolly sheep's costume was blocked by the people in front of her. When the angel appeared, Leslie remembered Holly mentioning the classmate who had gotten the part. It was obviously a case of typecasting since Sally Tuttle was an angelic-looking child with curly blond locks.

Tagg tilted his head slightly to murmur, "Holly could never look that innocent." It was an obvious reference to the girl playing the angel.

Leslie smiled briefly in acknowledgment, letting her hazel glance touch his profile. In a dark suit and tie, Tagg made a striking impression with his jet black hair, dark complexion and ice blue eyes. There was an air of maturity about him, travel and experience adding character to his handsomely chiseled features.

He had everything a girl could hope to find in a man—looks, personality, and sufficient wealth to be reasonably independent. Yet Leslie couldn't shake a sense of caution. She continued to hold back from any kind of commitment without being sure why she was. Some strong, protective instinct seemed to prevent it.

A choir of older members of the church class began singing Christmas hymns to bring the program to a close. The minister concluded with a brief prayer and an invitation for the parents and friends to partake of refreshments being served downstairs.

Still costumed, Holly met up with them in the church's small, outer lobby. "Can we stay?" she asked, wisps of black hair sticking out from her curly white hood with its floppy sheep ears. "They've got Christmas cookies and everything downstairs."

"Would you like to go down?" Tagg left the choice to Leslie and her aunt.

"Who can say no to Christmas cookies?" Patsy Evans asked and provided an affirmative answer with the question.

The refreshments were served in a small meeting room that quickly became crowded with children and adults. There was an empty space along the wall near the door where there was less chance of her crutches accidentally tripping someone. Leslie and her aunt waited there while Tagg and Holly brought them coffee and cookies.

As soon as Holly had eaten her cookies, she was lured away by some playmates. An acquaintance of Patsy Evans had drawn her off to one side to converse about a mutual friend, leaving Leslie and Tagg more or less standing alone.

The minister noticed them and came over. "Mr. Williams, I just wanted to tell you that I thought your daughter did a commendable job tonight. As a matter of fact, I don't have a 'baaaad' thing to say about it."

Leslie winced inwardly at the awful pun, but managed a smile.

"Thank you, Reverend August." Tagg pretended to smile, too. "I know Holly enjoyed it."

"Children are natural performers." The minister nodded and glanced curiously at Leslie. "Is this your wife? I don't believe I've had the pleasure of meeting her."

"Unfortunately she isn't my wife," Tagg corrected that impression. "This is Leslie Stiles."

"Of course." Her name produced instant recognition. "You are Mrs. Evans's niece, aren't you?"

"That's right." She nodded.

"I hope you'll forgive the mistake," the minister requested apologetically to both of them. "But when I saw the two of you standing together, it slipped my mind that you were a widower, Mr. Williams."

"No harm done," Tagg assured him.

Someone accidentally backed into her crutch, jostling Leslie's arm, and sloshing drops of coffee onto her white silk blouse. "Darn." She breathed out the

mild imprecation when she saw the stains. "Here."
She handed her cup to Tagg. "Hold this, will you?"

"Did you spill it on yourself?" he asked.

"Just a few drops," she admitted. "I should be able
to sponge them out with some cold water. Excuse
me, Reverend."

"Of course."

After she'd worked her way out of the room, she
went down the corridor to the ladies room. She managed to get the coffee stains out, leaving only a damp
spot on her blouse which wasn't too noticeable.

As she emerged from the ladies room, she heard
Holly's voice. She was playing in the corridor with
the Christmas angel, Sally Tuttle. Neither child
noticed Leslie coming up behind them.

"Who's that lady with your dad, Holly?" asked the
white-gowned girl with aluminum wings and halo.

"My mother," Holly replied with smooth non-
chalance, and Leslie went white.

"You told me you didn't have a mother," Sally
accused. "You said she died."

"She did, but that doesn't mean I can't have
another one," Holly insisted.

"Then how come this is the first time I've ever
seen her?" the girl challenged.

"Did you see her crutches? She has a broken leg
and she's been in the hospital. That's why she

hasn't been here before, so there!" Holly stuck out her tongue at her doubting friend.

"Holly!" Leslie spoke out sharply, realizing she should have stopped this before. She spun guiltily around and stared horror-struck at Leslie. "How can you say such a thing?" Leslie asked.

Something crumbled in her face. With a lowering chin, she turned back to the blond-haired Sally. "I made that all up. She isn't really my mother," Holly confessed stiffly. "But she could be." The last was issued in a kind of desperation.

"I knew she wasn't," Sally declared with a degree of smugness and went flouncing down the corridor.

Holly turned her round blue eyes at Leslie. "Are you mad 'cause I said that?"

"No, but you shouldn't say things that aren't true," Leslie said firmly. "Your friend would have found out sooner or later."

"I guess." She hung her head, scuffing the white toe of her shoe on the floor. "I'm sorry, Leslie."

"We'll forget about it this time." She was troubled by Holly's pretence. "But please, don't do it again."

"I won't," Holly promised with some reluctance.

"Let's go find your father and Aunt Patsy," Leslie suggested. "I think it's time we went home."

During the drive home, Holly was more subdued than usual although she did talk to Patsy Evans about the Christmas program and some of her new friends. Leslie hardly said anything at all.

The incident had merely added to her own inner doubts. In the past, Holly had always seemed so happy and content with her father that Leslie hadn't suspected the girl yearned for a woman's presence in her life. So much of the time she had spent in Tagg's company had included Holly. Now, anything that happened between them affected the child.

Leslie knew all about innocent victims. She had stood helplessly by while her parents had argued themselves into a divorce court, caught in the middle of a conflict that she didn't understand. She didn't want that to happen to Holly. She didn't want to inadvertently hurt her if she decided to stop seeing Tagg. And it was obviously nearing the point where Holly was becoming too attached to her.

When Tagg braked the car to a stop in the driveway, he asked, "Would you like to come inside for some hot chocolate?"

"Not me, thanks," her aunt refused. "It's time I was getting my beauty sleep."

"Leslie?" Tagg arched a brow at her.

She paused in the act of opening the car door. "No, I'll pass too. Thanks." Her aunt was already out of the car, but Leslie didn't wait for assistance from her or Tagg as she maneuvered out the side door on her own. She started down the sidewalk, following her aunt. Behind her, a car door was pushed shut as Tagg climbed out.

"Go into the house and get changed out of your costume," he told Holly, then called, "Leslie! Wait a minute."

She hesitated, then stopped to let him catch up with her, turning with a faint toss of her head. When he reached her side, his hands moved automatically onto her shoulders in a gesture that was possessive in its familiarity.

"Is something wrong?" He tipped his head to the side, his gaze probing.

"No. I've just got a headache." She took refuge in an old lie.

His gaze skimmed her, seeming to sense the falsehood, but he didn't press the issue. "Another time, then," he said.

"Yes." She accepted the ambiguous suggestion and smiled wanly. "Goodnight, Tagg."

She turned out of his arms and continued on her way to the house, conscious that he watched her for several long minutes before the sound of his footsteps carried him toward his own home. When she entered the kitchen, she pushed the door shut with her shoulder and leaned briefly against it, a troubled sigh sliding out with a long breath.

"Did you two have a lover's quarrel?" her aunt inquired bluntly, appearing without warning in the doorway.

"No." Her denial was cool and even. "And we aren't lovers."

"At a guess I'd say it isn't because Taggart isn't willing, so you must be the one holding back." Her aunt eyed her knowingly.

"I guess I'm not ready," Leslie shrugged.

"My dear girl, no one is ever ready to fall in love," her aunt informed her with a patient smile.

"I guess I'm not the exception," she declared with a wry and laughing shrug. "How about some tea?"

During the first three days of the week, Leslie only saw Tagg and Holly from the window of her aunt's house. She made no attempt to speak to them or make them aware of her presence. It wasn't easy, not as easy as she thought it would be. Tension wound around her until she thought she was going to snap.

After a restless night's sleep plagued by childhood nightmares, Leslie was late for breakfast. She swung into the kitchen on her crutches, an apology ready for oversleeping. It died on her lips when she saw Tagg sitting at the kitchen table drinking a cup of coffee.

"Good morning." His gaze was warm and bright with pleasure.

There was a curious singing in her ears, her spirits suddenly lifting despite her attempt to keep them on an even keel. "Good morning." She moved toward the table, glancing at her aunt. "Sorry I got up so late."

"I was going to come in and wake you when I heard you moving around. You have an appointment with my doctor this morning," Patsy reminded her.

"I'd forgotten." It had been made so long ago that it had completely slipped her mind, or been crowded out by too many other things. "What time am I supposed to be there?"

"Not until eleven. Don't worry. You have plenty of time," she assured, then cast a short glance at Taggart Williams. "As a matter of fact, Taggart said he'd be happy to take you to the doctor's office for your checkup. I think there's something he wants to show you, too."

"Something to show me?" Leslie repeated with a slight frown.

"That's why I came over this morning. I was going to take you by so you could see what you thought about it."

"You found a puppy for Holly," Leslie guessed.

"I found a puppy for Holly, but that isn't what I want you to see. Will you come?" Tagg asked. "It's right on the way to the doctor's."

"I—" She wanted to go with him, so why deny it? "I'll come."

There was only time for a light breakfast of coffee and toast. She changed quickly to a better outfit, then left to accompany Tagg in his car. Even though curiosity was getting the better of her, she refused to ask where he was taking her or what he wanted her to see.

Tagg was equally uncommunicative, not giving her any hints or clues about their destination. When he reversed out of the driveway, he made the turn toward town.

# CHAPTER

# 9

TAGG PARKED THE car in front of an empty building located around the corner from the town's main street. She gave him a puzzled look.

"This is it?" she asked skeptically.

"Yup." He nodded his head toward the empty building. "What do you think of it?"

"It's a building. What am I supposed to think of it?"

His tongue clicked in mock reproval. "I should hope you would think something. You are looking at the future offices of Taggart J. Williams, Attorney-at-Law." His smile came quick and disturbing. "Come on. I want to show you inside."

Without giving her a chance to disagree, he climbed out of the car and walked around to help her over the snowdrift to the sidewalk. The lock stubbornly resisted his key and gave in after a few hard shakes of the doorknob.

A bare bulb hung from the ceiling of the small anteroom. There was no furniture or drapes to alleviate the bareness of the walls and windows. The building didn't give the appearance of having been used in a long time.

"It needs painting and some minor renovations," Tagg admitted as if reading her thoughts. "But I thought this could be used as the reception area. There's three more rooms back here."

Pausing to switch on the lights, he led the way through the inner door into a short hall with three doors branching off of it. He opened the one on his right and let Leslie enter another bare room.

"I thought this could be used for the secretary. There's room for her desk and some filing cabinets," he explained. "I'm going to have a carpenter cut an opening in the wall to connect this with the reception area so she can see whoever comes in."

One glance around the four bare walls took in all there was to see. Leslie had an impression of a comfortably sized office with adequate work space and floor space. Then Tagg was directing her into the hallway once more.

"This room is too small to be used for anything

but storage of supplies and files," he said, opening the door to the room across the hall and letting her glimpse inside. "Down here will be my office."

It was the largest of the three rooms, but also the one in most need of repair. The ceiling was water-stained, indicating the roof had leaked at some point. The paint was peeling off the walls, the plaster chipped in places.

"Most of this wall space can be used for shelves for all my law books—a kind of legal library," Tagg mocked. "The rest of the walls can be paneled. All I have to do is find a big oak desk and some maroon leather furniture and I'll be in the law business." He swung around to face her, his hands slid inside her coat onto the curves of her waist. "What do you think of it?"

"It seems ideal," she agreed. "Of course, it's going to take some work to fix it up."

"It won't take long once I get the carpenters and painters in here." His hands moved further around her waist to link together at the small of her back. Bending his head, he brushed his mouth over her cheekbone. The light caress trapped a breath in her throat. "I've got to start looking for a secretary." He rubbed his mouth over her lips, then straightened to look at her. "Have you ever given any thought to becoming a legal secretary?"

"No." It came out on that trapped breath.

"The salary probably wouldn't be as high as what you're being paid now, but you can't beat the fringe benefits that go along with the job," he insisted lazily. "What do you think?"

"I—" Leslie dragged her gaze down to the top button of his parka, staring at it and trying to make her heart return to its normal beat. "I already have a job."

She felt the stillness that went through him and the hard probe of his eyes, which she wouldn't meet. The silence ran for long seconds, growing heavier.

"Leslie—" Tagg began.

"Hellooo!" A voice called from the front of the building. "Anybody here!"

Tagg swore savagely under his breath and let go of Leslie, stepping away. "Yes! What is it?" His reply was short-tempered as he moved to the hall door where footsteps approached.

"Tagg Williams?" An older man in a business suit and topcoat appeared.

"Yes," he nodded, his eyes narrowed in sharp question for the man to state his business.

"You don't know me, but I was a great admirer of your father—the Judge." He reached out to shake Tagg's hand. "I was over to Bill Yates's store. He told me you had leased this building to open your law practice and said that was your car parked out front. My name's Davis Long."

"Mr. Long. I believe I remember my father mentioning your name." Tagg frowned as if trying to recall. "You're a banker."

"That's right." A smile widened his face, surprised and pleased. "Since I was here, I wanted to stop by and make myself known to you. Banks are always in need of legal advice. When you open your practice, I hope you'll come by and discuss the possibility of acting as counsel for us."

"It would be my pleasure," Tagg assured him.

"I won't keep you any longer," the man stated with a quick glance at Leslie. "I know you're busy. Welcome back to Vermont." He took a business card from his pocket and handed it to Tagg.

"Thank you. I'll be in touch," he promised.

For a long moment, there was only the retreating echo of the banker's footsteps as he retraced his route to the door. Tagg looked at the card and slipped it inside his pocket.

"My first prospective client." There was a sardonic note in his voice as he turned and glanced at Leslie.

"And you haven't officially opened your doors." Her attempt at a bright response came out stiff.

His glance ran over her, searching and testing before sliding away without finding what he wanted.

"We'd better get started to the clinic or you'll be late for your appointment."

It was a short, but silent drive to the medical clinic. Tagg seemed preoccupied, an absent frown creasing his forehead.

Almost as soon as they arrived, Leslie was ushered into an examining room. It had been simpler to have all her medical records forwarded to her aunt's physician than to make the drive all the way back to New York to see her doctor. It was merely a routine checkup to make sure her leg was mending nicely.

The doctor was a young, bearded man named Hornsby. After he'd finished his examination, he picked up her chart. "How long has this cast been on? Five weeks?"

"Yes," Leslie nodded.

"How would you like an early Christmas present?" he asked.

"I beg your pardon?"

"From everything I've seen today, the bone has healed. There's no reason why your cast can't be taken off a week early," he explained.

"That's wonderful news." But she didn't feel as elated as she thought she would. Like Tagg and his first prospective client, she couldn't get excited about her cast being removed either.

It was a strangely naked feeling when she limped into the waiting room without the cast and crutches, supported with the aid of a cane. Surprise pierced the aloofness of Tagg's expression when he noticed her freed leg.

"Congratulations," he said.

"I feel as if I've lost twenty pounds," she admitted.

Suddenly they both ran out of things to say. The silence was back, thickening until it seemed impenetrable.

"I guess we'd better go," Leslie suggested finally. "Holly will be getting out of school soon."

"Right." It was a grim sound, like his expression as Tagg escorted her outside to the car.

When they drove onto the highway, Leslie stared out the side window. She didn't see the mud-spattered snowbanks along the road. She didn't see anything. Tension knotted her stomach into a tight band.

His sudden braking startled her. She looked around, thinking they were about to hit something. But the road before them was free of traffic. Tagg shifted the car into reverse and backed up to turn into a lay-by.

"Why are we stopped?" She frowned at him.

Both hands rested on top of the wheel as the engine idled, keeping warm air blowing into the car's interior. Tagg breathed in deeply, then turned his head to study her hard.

"Because we need to talk," he stated. "What's the matter, Leslie? Have I been taking too much for granted?"

"I think so." She nodded, lowering her chin.

Shifting his position, he sat sideways in the seat, his arm lying along the back. Without any advance signal of his intention, Tagg leaned over and caught her chin between his fingers, lifting it so his mouth could cover her lips. His kiss was roughly demanding, licking through her like heat lightning.

Her fingers curled into the virile thickness of his hair in a response she was helpless to deny. There was a potency of feeling in his embrace that made her overlook other considerations. When she finally dragged her lips from the moistness of his, she lowered her head in a shaky reaction.

"Do you expect me to believe that when you kiss me like that, it means nothing?" Tagg demanded in a voice thickened by his disturbed state. "Why won't you admit it? Are you afraid?"

"I'm terrified," she whispered.

"Of what?" He pulled back, a darkening frown gathering on his features.

"Of you—of me. Of being wrong," Leslie admitted.

"So you aren't going to take the chance of finding out it's right?" he challenged angrily.

"You seem to be forgetting about your daughter," she retorted, her temper flaring from the sparks of his. "At church the other night, she was telling her friend that I was her mother. If I hadn't come along, who knows how many more of her friends she might have decided to tell."

"Holly did that?" he frowned skeptically.

"Yes."

"I've never known her to make up stories," he insisted.

"Well, she did. I was surprised, too, but I realized how easily she can be hurt. I know what it's like to want something so badly that it hurts inside. You pretend to yourself and others, hoping that if you pretend hard enough it will come true."

"Your parents," he guessed.

"Yes, my parents. The situation isn't the same. I know that. But I wanted so desperately for them to be happy together—for all of us to be happy—instead of constantly shouting and yelling." All the old hurt was back, twisting at her heart and squeezing her chest until it was difficult to breathe. "Even when they separated, which they did many times, I wanted them to get back together. I wanted it to all work out right—the way it did in the books." She stopped, lowering her head. "But it didn't. It still hasn't." There was a hint of moisture in her eyes when she looked at Tagg. "I don't want Holly to start hoping for something that might never be."

"Leslie." Involuntarily Tagg muttered her name and closed his eyes, a taut frustration hardening his features.

His hold tightened to gather her against his chest, his fingers burrowing into her hair to press her head to his shoulder, as he tried to comfort her and take away her fears. She trembled, haunted by the ghosts of things past, and shut her eyes to let the sensations of his solid warmth claim her. His head was bent to her, the side of his jaw, chin, and mouth rubbing against her forehead in an absent caress.

"It's perfectly normal for Holly to want a mother." His low voice was thick with tautly checked emotion. "I'd be more worried if she didn't. Instead of being upset that she picked you for the role, you should be flattered. It's quite a compliment when someone chooses you to be their parent, even if it's only pretend."

"I know," Leslie whispered, but that wasn't the point.

"God knows I approve of her choice," Tagg muttered as he turned his mouth against her face, trailing rough kisses over her eyebrows and temples.

His fingers tightened in her hair, gently tugging her head back so he could find her lips. They parted under his hungry pressure, the blood drumming in her ears. She strained toward him, wanting to be absorbed into him forever and escape these doubts.

Equally frustrated in his attempts to feel her against him, Tagg let go of her briefly and shifted his hold to pull her across his lap where there was no more awkwardness of position. Her arms went around his neck and shoulders as she came back to seek the heady stimulation of his drugging kiss.

With his arm supporting her shoulders and back, his hand pushed its way inside her coat, spreading across her waist and ribs to feel and caress with roaming interest. Desire fevered her flesh with raw and wild longings as she sought the excitement of his tongue, deepening the kiss with fierce pleasure.

There was a growing pressure in her loins, a need for assuagement. It swelled within her, expanding her breast under the cupping caress of his hand. He dragged his mouth from her lips to graze along the skin of her throat. She tipped her head back to allow him greater access, a moaning sigh coming from her lips.

There were too many clothes, too many layers of material to give either of them the closeness they desired. Their temperatures were rising. Between their combined body heat and the warm air blowing from the heater vents and their own passion, the windows were steamed over. Leslie could taste the perspiration on his skin.

When his hand invaded her sweater, it was prepared for the camisole she wore underneath and slipped under the loose garment to glide onto the naked skin of her breast. She shuddered under the sensual stimulation of his stroking thumb, circling the hard point.

His mouth returned to her lips to mutter against them, "I didn't intend for this to happen when we met, any more than you did. But it has. You can't change it." The moistness of his breath was in her mouth, filling every hidden corner.

"I know." The attraction was too strong. It wouldn't be ruled by caution, but it was its very strength that troubled her.

He dragged his hand away from her breast, faint tremors quaking through him as he made a shaky attempt to control his desires. Lifting his head, Tagg traced his fingers over her flushed and softened features. His expression was taut, a nerve twitching in his jaw while his searching gaze probed with a tearing earnestness.

"I've done everything but come right out and say it, Leslie," Tagg murmured. "Before a man tells a woman he loves her, he likes to have some indication that she feels the same. When you offer someone your heart, you don't want them to refuse it. You said I was rushing you, so I've waited. How much longer is it going to be?"

"I don't know." They were troubled words coming from a wary heart.

His mouth tightened. "All right, I'll say it then. I love you."

She looked at him with a sad skepticism that challenged. "How can you be sure?"

His breath came out in a short, humorless laugh, as if concealing his hurt at her doubt. "Well, I don't hear any bells ringing and I haven't noticed any fireworks displays, but I know what I feel. It's love."

"But you were wrong once before," Leslie reminded him in a quietly reluctant voice. "You separated from your first wife . . . and only reconciled after you found out about Holly. You must have known a child can't hold a marriage together once it's fallen apart."

"Yes, I knew there was only a remote chance that my marriage to Cindy could be salvaged," Tagg admitted with a hard glitter in his blue eyes, a hint of impatient anger showing. "But I owed it to our unborn child to find out, didn't I?"

"Yes," she conceded that point. "But you must

have thought you were in love with her, too, when you married her. If you were mistaken then, you could be mistaken now."

"I made a mistake—once." He stressed the last word. "Does that mean I'm not entitled to another chance?"

"It means you could be wrong again," Leslie murmured.

"I'm not," he stated. "There isn't any way I can prove it. You'll just have to believe me. Part of loving a person is trusting them."

"That isn't easy." Her protective instinct was too strong; there were too many scars and too much potential for more pain for her to lightly accept his word. Leslie shifted out of his arms and moved to her own side of the car seat, straightening her coat. The silence grew, finally pulling her glance to Tagg.

"Love doesn't come easy—not the kind that lasts," he said quietly. "It requires work and effort from both parties involved. It only *seems* to happen on its own. I think you love me but you're afraid of it. You have to be willing to take that last step. I can't take it for you."

He didn't seem to expect a reply from her as he shifted out of parking gear to drive onto the road. Instinctively Leslie knew that he was speaking the truth. Yet it didn't ease any of her misgivings. Tagg believed he loved her but did he? Until she was sure, how could she risk taking that last step?

Turning into the driveway to her aunt's house, he stopped the car and let the engine idle. "I have to pick up Holly at school," Tagg said to explain why he was letting her out here.

"Of course," she reached for the door handle, but his hand on her arm stayed her.

When she looked back, he leaned across the intervening space and kissed her, tasting the soft curves of her lips and lingering on them for a moist second before drawing back. "I'll see you Christmas Eve."

His remark had the sound of a deadline, that she had to make up her mind by then or lose him. She silently railed at the unfairness of putting a time limit as she climbed out of the car, moving more freely without the cumbersome cast. A threading and weaving tension wound through her nerves when she watched him reverse out of the driveway.

"Merry Christmas! Merry Christmas!" Holly chimed the happy greeting to Leslie and her aunt in turn as she bounded into the kitchen, almost running Leslie down when she opened the door. "You should see all the stars in the sky. Santa Claus won't need to have Rudolph show him the way tonight," she declared.

After avoiding a collision with the red-bundled whirlwind of Christmas cheer, Leslie swung her attention to the man who followed, too conscious of the hinted deadline to listen to Holly's mythical observations. By then, Tagg was almost beside her.

"Merry Christmas." His swooping mouth kissed her startled lips with tormenting swiftness and moved away. An eyebrow danced above sparkling blue eyes. "Mmm, that was nice. Maybe I should try it again."

"Tagg." She was stunned, in a delightfully reluctant way, by his boldness in stealing a kiss not only in front of Holly but her aunt as well.

He chuckled at her halfhearted protest and came the rest of the way into the kitchen. "Merry Christmas, Mrs. Evans."

"Merry Christmas. What's this? Presents?" her aunt declared, drawing Leslie's glance to the gift-wrapped packages Tagg carried.

"Just a little something from Holly and me." He shrugged lightly and handed them to her while he took off his coat.

Holly had already scrambled out of hers. "Why don't you open them now?" she urged the woman. "One's for you and one's for Leslie."

"Why don't we all go into the living room by the fireplace?" her aunt suggested. "I believe I remember seeing a present in there with your name on it and we can open them together."

"With my name on it?" Holly asked with wide-eyed wonder. "Really?"

"Yes. Come. I'll show you." Patsy Evans curved a hand on the little girl's shoulder to guide her into the living room.

Which left Leslie to walk with Tagg. Although her leg was still weak, the exercises she'd been doing since the cast had been removed had strengthened it so it could bear her weight without relying on the cane. She still favored it, walking with a slight limp. Tagg's hand rested on her waist, for support if she needed it.

In the living room, Tagg guided her to the sofa and sat on the cushion next to her, casually resting his arm along the back. When Patsy Evans handed a rectangular-shaped gift to her, Leslie was reluctant to unwrap it, thinking it might in some way compromise her position. Instead she watched Holly eagerly tearing away the paper on her present.

When she lifted out the books, she held them up for Tagg to see. "Look, Daddy. Books." She was obviously pleased with the gift. "I haven't read either one of them before." Then she noticed Leslie hadn't opened her present. "Hurry up, Leslie, so you can see what book we bought you. Whoops!" She clamped a hand over her mouth. "I wasn't supposed to tell."

"I still don't know which book it is," Leslie assured her, sliding a finger under the tape to loosen it from the paper. Inwardly, she was relieved to have some idea of what the package contained.

In the meantime, her aunt had opened her gift. "A collection of poems by Robert Frost—and one I don't have. Thank you."

Underneath the Christmas paper and ribbon, there was a leather-bound edition of A Christmas Carol by Charles Dickens. A smile of amused disbelief wavered on Leslie's face.

"Daddy said you liked the hero of that book," Holly explained and waited for Leslie to confirm that it had been an appropriate choice.

"It's one of my favorites by Dickens," she said.

"I thought it would be good bedtime reading for Christmas Eve," Tagg murmured, a wicked light glittering in his eyes.

"Without a doubt," Leslie agreed, unable to keep the amusement out of her voice.

"I'm going to start reading my books now," Holly declared and opened up the first one to begin reading aloud.

All three of them became involved, helping her with the words she didn't know. When the story reached a point where it could be stopped, Patsy Evans suggested it would be a good time to put the book aside and have their supper. Everyone lent a hand in the kitchen to carry the crackers and bowls of steaming oyster stew into the dining room.

"I almost forgot to tell you." Holly was trailing after Patsy Evans with a bowl of little, round oyster crackers. "Do you know what I heard when we were coming over here to your house? I heard Santa's sleigh flying high in the sky."

Tagg leaned his head toward Leslie and murmured, for her ears alone, "It sounded very much like a puppy whining because it doesn't like being in the garage all alone."

"Of course, that's not what it was," she said dryly, guessing he had smuggled Holly's Christmas puppy into the garage.

"It had to be the whine of Santa's sleigh," he insisted with a wink.

After supper was finished, Tagg and Holly didn't stay long. As he explained, they opened their gifts on Christmas Eve so there would be room under the tree for the presents Santa brought.

"And I have to go to bed early tonight," Holly added. " 'Cause Santa only comes when you're sleeping."

Leslie was about to conclude that Tagg was not going to raise the issue of their last conversation.

But while her aunt was helping Holly into her coat, Tagg drew her to one side.

"Have you thought about what we discussed?" There was a watchful quality in his gaze.

"Yes." It was nearly all she'd thought about.

"And?" Tagg prompted.

"I'm still thinking," she said.

There was an uneasy quavering in her stomach as she watched him breathe in deeply. A smile of reluctant acceptance finally edged his mouth to show his continued patience with her. When Leslie smiled, it was out of relief that he hadn't been setting a deadline, giving her a now-or-never kind of ultimatum.

When he bent to kiss her, she ignored the fact there were spectators and kissed him back. For a second, it almost got out of hand, then her aunt cleared her throat and they drew apart, exchanging intimate and self-conscious looks.

"It's a shame Santa has such a busy night ahead of him," Tagg murmured.

"Yes, it is," she agreed.

"I'm ready to go, Dad," Holly hurried him along.

# CHAPTER

# 10

EARLY ON CHRISTMAS morning, there was a loud pounding at the kitchen door. Leslie was still in her quilted robe, not having taken the time to dress before her first cup of coffee. She set the freshly poured cup on the counter and limped to the door in her furry brown slippers.

Holly was standing outside, both arms wrapped around a wiggling ball of white and brown fur. She was wearing the biggest smile Leslie had ever seen as she stepped into the kitchen to show off her new puppy.

"Look what Santa Claus brought me." She offered the puppy to Leslie so she could hold it. Its pink little tongue immediately began washing her face, a fluffy bundle of love. "His name is Chris. That's short for Christmas, 'cause that's when I got him."

"He's beautiful," Leslie laughed, managing to get the squirming pup away from her face so she could elude its licking kisses. When she glimpsed its long, thin nose, she guessed that it belonged to either the shepherd or the collie breed.

"When I came downstairs this morning, there was a big box under the tree," she explained. "I went over and looked inside—and there he was. There was a big red bow around his neck, but he chewed it off. I guess it tickled him. When he saw me, he got all excited—just like he knew he belonged to me."

"I'll bet that's because he knew you would love him." Leslie handed the puppy back to Holly and smiled at the way she hugged with such affection. It whined with excitement.

"I just had to come over so you could see Chris," Holly said, wanting to share the joy of this moment. She glanced beyond Leslie. "Aunt Patsy, look what Santa brought me."

The explanations started all over again as she showed the puppy to Leslie's aunt. She made all the suitable comments about what a fine-looking animal it was.

"Is this what you asked Santa to bring you?" her aunt inquired, rubbing the puppy's ears.

"Well, I did ask him for something else," Holly admitted with a thoughtful frown. "But I guess Santa can only bring certain kinds of things like toys and puppies. I'm glad I've got Christmas."

"So am I." Patsy smiled. "You'll have to take real good care of him."

"I will. Santa even brought dog food and dishes for his water and his puppy food." She turned suddenly to Leslie. "I almost forgot. Santa Claus left a present for you at our house."

"What?" A startled frown flickered across her face.

"I told you that you should have a tree," Holly reminded her with a knowing nod of her head. "Since you didn't have one, Santa had to leave your present under our tree. He knew we'd make sure you got it."

"I think there must be a mistake—" Leslie made a confused protest.

"No. Santa doesn't make a mistake," Holly insisted. "Daddy looked at the package and said it had your name on it. I'm supposed to tell you to come over and get it."

"I'll come over later—" she began.

"No, come over now," Holly coaxed. "I want to see what Santa brought you."

"But I'm not dressed." She glanced down at her quilted lounging robe in a chocolate brown trimmed with gold ribbing.

189

"Nonsense, you have more clothes on than you usually do," her aunt scoffed at that excuse. "You're covered from head to foot. Just throw a coat on and go over."

"Yes, Leslie. Please." Holly pleaded. "There isn't any snow on the walk and the sun is out."

"All right." She gave into their urgings, but she was conscious of her heart racing.

After donning her coat, she followed Holly outside. It was a bright Christmas morning with the sunlight glinting off the snow. Holly put the puppy on the ground and the pair of them ran ahead of the limping Leslie.

By the time she reached the front porch steps, Holly had the door open and was announcing her arrival. "Daddy! Leslie's here to get her present from Santa."

When she entered the house, she saw him standing in the living room, a coffee cup in his hand. He was dressed in a long-sleeved, flannel shirt in a gray and black plaid and gray corduroy slacks. There was a faint accusation in her glance when she met the knowing glitter of his gaze.

"Your present's under the tree." He used the cup to motion in the direction of the tree.

There was only one square package under the tree, so there could be no doubt which was hers.

Her leg was tired and beginning to ache; her limp was more noticeable as she approached the tree.

"Maybe you'd better sit down," Tagg suggested and pushed the ottoman closer to the tree.

She sank gratefully onto it, conscious of him towering beside her. The puppy romped about her feet in uncoordinated play while Holly hovered anxiously behind Leslie as she picked up the lightweight box wrapped in silver foil.

"This isn't fair," she said stiffly to Tagg, sliding him an irritated glance. "I didn't buy you anything."

"Don't look at me." He drew back in mock innocence. "This present is from Santa Claus."

"Oh, hurry up and open it, Leslie," Holly urged impatiently. "I want to see."

When she removed the emerald green ribbon, the puppy grabbed it and began chewing and tearing it to shreds. He pounced on the silver foil, too, when it fell to the floor. Leslie slipped off the lid and began lifting aside the tissue that protected the contents. She just kept encountering more tissue.

"What's inside?" Holly was leaning over her shoulder, trying to see into the box.

"A lot of tissue." Then her fingers felt a second small box inside.

Her gaze darted to Tagg as she slowly lifted it out.

He silently held her glance. She could hear the thudding of her heart as she stared at the ring box.

"Another box!" Holly exclaimed with delight. "Open it up, Leslie."

There was a tightness in her throat. Very slowly, she pushed back the hinged lid. Nestled on a bed of blue velvet sat a diamond ring, a solitaire in the center with smaller diamonds designed around it in the shape of a five-pronged star.

"Ooooh!" Holly was awed by the thousands of lights that sparkled from the diamond cuts. "It's beautiful."

Leslie didn't say a thing, her breath coming painfully shallow. There was the sting of tears in her eyes. Her fingers tightened their hold on the box, her knuckles turning white under the pressure.

"It looks just like the Christmas star, doesn't it, Daddy?" Holly declared in amazement. "It sparkles brighter than anything."

"Yes, it does." His voice was calmly quiet, but to Leslie, it seemed to come from some great distance. "Now that you've seen it, why don't you take your puppy outside?"

"Okay." Holly needed no second urging, unconcerned by Leslie's silence. "Come here, Christmas!" she called the bounding puppy to her side and scooped it into her arms. "We've got to go outside so you don't make any messes in the house. You've got to learn to be a good puppy."

All the while Leslie seemed to be frozen in position. It wasn't until the front door closed and there was silence in the room that she finally lifted her gaze by degrees to Tagg. There was a mute appeal in the shimmer of her hazel eyes. He ignored it and took a sip of his coffee.

"There's a card inside," he said. "Why don't you read it?"

This time her fingers were trembling when they searched through the tissue-filled box and came up with a small white card. There was a message written on it in a neatly lettered scroll.

"There is a man who loves you very much," it read. "I would appreciate your assistance and ask that you wear this ring so he may have the Christmas present he wants."

It was signed: *Santa Claus*.

Moisture collected in her eyes, blurring the words when she tried to read them a second time. She was shaking inside, deeply moved by his touching ploy. Yet she remained in the grip of her silence.

Tagg crouched down in front of her, the study of his gaze becoming intense. "Am I going to get my present?"

Her head made a slow move from side to side,

but it wasn't a gesture of denial. It was an expression of helplessness. With all her heart, she wanted to give him the answer he sought but that fear of making a mistake held her motionless.

"I want you to marry me, Leslie," Tagg said huskily. "I want you to be my wife."

She looked again at the ring. A star of hope. A star of love. A Christmas star shining out at her from a heaven of blue velvet.

"I want to marry you," Leslie admitted in a wavering voice that was still not an acceptance.

"I haven't made it a habit of proposing to women. You're the first one I've asked since Cindy died. I don't mean to sound like I'm bragging, but I've been with a fair number of women in the interim—and there were willing takers among them if I'd asked. But I didn't ask because I didn't love them. I know the difference."

"I'm sorry." Her voice trembled, because she didn't mean for her doubt to be interpreted as a belief he treated the vows of marriage lightly.

"I understand why you are wary," Tagg said. "Your parents' divorce must have been a painful and traumatic experience for you. But I also went through it—as one of the parties directly involved, not just an innocent victim as you were. It isn't something I want to go through again either."

The shaking stopped as she slowly lifted her gaze to him. She searched his face, suddenly realizing she had not considered what he had been through. Foolishly she had been thinking that she was the only one who knew the agony of a broken marriage.

"Christmas is all about God and love. It's something you can't see or touch, but you have to have faith. You have to believe in love," he stated.

It was all so simple when put in that context. Leslie could almost feel the peace stealing over her as she accepted what he said. With new calmness and confidence in what lay ahead, she removed the star ring from its box and gave it to Tagg.

"Would you put it on my finger?" she asked, finding it suddenly so easy to take that last step.

It was as if he had braced himself for something else. For a pounding moment, Tagg could only stare at her, not quite believing she meant it. But her left hand was extended to him, steady and sure.

His expression became filled with highly charged emotion, a bursting of wild joy and inexpressible pride. He gripped her hand and slid the ring on her finger. Both of them looked at it, sparkling there with a radiant light that seemed to shine with the fullness of their love.

When he swept her into his arms and crushed her mouth under his, happiness spilled through her like a raging torrent. All the doubts and fears were washed away by the flood of emotion. His mouth bruised her with his desire, but the pain was exquisitely sweet.

Dazed by the radiant joy that claimed her, Leslie was certain she heard bells ringing, muffled and far away, but it sounded very much like them. She wondered if she wasn't a little bit crazy when the kiss finally ended and Tagg held her tightly in his arms.

"I can't believe it," she murmured.

"Believe what?" he asked thickly, drawing his head back to look at her.

Her fingers stroked his strong features in a tactile exploration. "I actually thought I heard bells." She lazily studied his mouth, fascinated by its firm line and latent sexuality.

It quirked. "You did."

"What?" There was a lilt of absent curiosity in her voice, too, intrigued by little discoveries to pay close attention to words when actions were more satisfying.

"You did hear bells," Tagg repeated. "They were the church bells ringing out the message of Christmas."

She laughed and traced a finger under his jaw. "Just think—we can tell our children that I heard bells the day you proposed to me."

His eyes darkened with smoldering desire. "I

want you, Leslie. I want you. I want your children. I want your love for the rest of my life and beyond."

The smile left her face as Leslie looked at him with sober intensity. "And I want you and your children—and your love for the rest of my life and beyond. Because I love you, Tagg." She finally said the words that no other man had heard, the ones she'd saved so they would have meaning and commitment behind them.

As his mouth moved onto hers, her fingers curled themselves into his hair, the star diamond ring winking its light in the blackness. The driving force of his kiss pressed her backward on the ottoman while his restless hand traveled over the point of her hip and the curve of her waist, caressing and stimulating.

The slam of the front door sent a draft of cold air blowing over the intertwining bodies. There was no time to sit up or disguise the passionate embrace before Holly dashed into the room with the awkwardly galloping puppy at her heels. It was all done after she was there.

Leslie's cheeks were flushed with an embarrassed heat, and Tagg noted the face with amusement. To avoid Holly's wide-eyed stare of curiosity, Leslie made a show of straightening her robe and brushing back the ends of her hair.

"What are you doing, Daddy?" Holly asked.

"I was kissing Leslie," he said candidly and reached out an arm to draw his daughter to his side.

"You kissed her the morning after we'd slept in front of the fireplace, but it wasn't like that," she said.

"That was a good morning kiss. There are different kinds of kisses," Tagg explained, more accustomed to fielding such questions than Leslie was.

"What kind of kiss was that?" Holly asked, meaning the one she had interrupted.

"That's the way a man kisses a woman when they are going to get married—and after they get married," he added the last as an advance warning of other kisses to come that "big eyes" might see.

"Are you going to marry Leslie?" She seemed to hold her breath.

"Yes." Tagg reached to clasp Leslie's hand, the one with the ring.

"And when you marry her, she'll be my mommy, won't she?" Holly asked, excitement beginning to bubble from her.

"Yes."

"I did get my present from Santa!" She began jumping up and down. "I did! I wanted Leslie to be my mother more than anything! I thought Santa couldn't bring me a present like that."

"I didn't know anything about this." Tagg

frowned and looked at his daughter curiously. "How come you didn't tell me?"

"Because—I didn't want to tell anybody," Holly declared. "I was afraid Santa wouldn't do it. That's why I wrote him the letter all by myself."

"The letter I mailed to Santa Claus," Leslie realized.

"Yes, that's the one," she admitted with a quick nod of her head. "Now you're going to be with us all the time—every minute. And you won't be staying at Aunt Patsy's any more."

"Whoa! Wait a minute before you damage my future wife's reputation." Tagg called a halt to Holly's opinion of how it was going to be. "Before Leslie can stay with us all the time, there has to be a wedding."

"How would you like to be one of my bridesmaids, Holly?" Leslie asked.

"Can I?" she asked excitedly.

"I wouldn't want anyone else." She smiled.

"When can we have the wedding?" Holly wanted to know. "Can we have it tomorrow—on my birthday?"

"No, not tomorrow," Tagg chuckled. "Not that it wouldn't be nice, but it takes a little longer than that to arrange a wedding. But it will be soon."

"Boy, just wait until I tell Sally Tuttle that you're going to be my mother!" Holly exclaimed. "I can hardly wait until the vacation's over and school starts." A thought suddenly occurred to her. "If Leslie is going to be my mother, then Aunt Patsy is really going to be my aunt."

"That's right," Leslie nodded.

"Can I go tell her?" She was bursting to tell someone.

"Sure. Why not?" Leslie laughed softly.

In a flash, Holly was out the door and racing down the porch steps to run next door and break the news. With a hopeless shake of his head, Tagg turned back to Leslie and kissed the ring on her hand.

"It seems both Holly and me got our present from Santa Claus," he murmured and started to draw her back into his arms.

She snuggled into his arms, enfolded in their warmth and his love. "Why did you pretend my ring was a present from Santa Claus?" she asked. "Why didn't you simply propose to me?"

"How could anyone turn down Santa Claus?" Tagg countered, murmuring the question against her hair.

"That isn't an answer," she declared with amused reproach.

"Because I wanted you to believe in the goodness of Santa Claus and to know that he gives from the heart. He's love and he lives in the heart."

"Christmas is going to be my favorite time of the

year from now on," Leslie sighed in contentment. "In the past, it has been such an unhappy season. Until this year when I came here and met you. Now it's the happiest."

"I still remember how you looked that day when you helped Holly make the paper chain for the tree." Amusement riddled his voice. "You were so indignant when I said I believed in Santa Claus. I expected any minute to be accused of corrupting my daughter with fairy-tale nonsense."

"If Holly hadn't been there, I probably would have," she admitted, remembering well how she had scorned any perpetuation of the Santa Claus myth.

"Indignant and so vulnerable," he murmured. "It was an intriguing combination. You tried to be so tough—and so cynical."

"You made me laugh at myself, and not take everything quite so seriously," Leslie realized.

"All of us have to believe in Santa Claus and Peter Pan. We need to keep a bit of a child's faith," Tagg said.

"I can see that now," she agreed.

"And you can see that I love you and want you to be my wife." The roughness of need was in his voice, making it husky. "How soon can we set the wedding date?"

"I've been thinking about that," Leslie admitted

with a faintly troubled sigh. "Naturally my father is going to want to give me away. And if he comes, my mother won't."

"That's easily fixed," Tagg told her. "We'll elope—and not invite either of them."

"Tagg," she said in a reproving tone.

"I'm serious," he insisted. "There aren't going to be any undercurrents of unhappiness on our wedding day. After we're married we'll fly to Baltimore to see your mother, then honeymoon in Hawaii and see your father."

"It sounds wonderful," Leslie agreed and wrapped his arms a little tighter around her. "What about Holly? Are we going to take her along?"

"I love my daughter very much but I have no intention of taking her on my honeymoon," he stated without hesitation. "There will be plenty of opportunities in the future for us to vacation together as a family. This trip will be ours alone."

"Maybe Aunt Patsy will look after her," she suggested the possibility. "I think Holly would like that. And my aunt seems to have become quite fond of her."

"We'll ask, but either way, we'll make some kind of arrangements to have the time alone," Tagg answered her. "When we get back, that will be soon enough for you to assume the responsibility of being a mother."

"And a legal secretary?" she teased.

"I'll make sure your duties are light," he promised. "I know what a demanding husband you'll have at home."

"And how demanding is that?" It was a deliberately provocative challenge, fully aware that Tagg would show her, and he did.

Here's an exciting look
at four novels from
one of Janet Dailey's most
beloved series:
The Calders

*This Calder Range*
*Stands a Calder Man*
*This Calder Sky*
*Calder Born, Calder Bred*

All available from Pocket Books

# This Calder Range

# SEPTEMBER 1878

# 1

IT WAS A COUNTRY of benchlands and breaks, coulees and cutbanks—and grass that stretched a hundred miles in every direction. The dominating expanse of blue sky overhead seemed to flatten it, but this vast northern range undulated like a heavy sea. The lonely grandeur of it gripped at the heart of the strong and intimidated the weak.

A pair of riders leading packhorses topped a crest of this virgin Montana Territory and reined in. From the stout, double-rigged saddle to the shotgun chaps and the low crown of their cowboy hats, their clothes and their gear marked them as Texans. They were covered with a thick layer of travel dust.

They walked their horses partway down the gentle slope and stopped again when they were no longer skylined by the plain's swell. Saddle leather groaned as the taller of the two men swung to the ground in a fluid motion. The chalk-faced bay he was riding blew out a snort and dipped its nose toward the grass.

Rawboned and lean, Chase Benteen Calder carried his near-six-foot height with the ease of a shorter man. His weight was distributed in hard muscles that lay flatly across his chest and broad shoulders and the long girth of his legs. The twenty-six years of his life had beaten a toughness into his boldly spaced features. It showed in the quickness of his dark eyes, the small break along the bridge of his nose, and the pale track of an old scar on his right temple. Experience had made him closemouthed and vigilant, and the sun had darkened him.

He kept a hold on the reins to his chalk-faced bay while it lowered its head to graze. The rattle of the bridle bit briefly drew his glance to the horse tearing at the curly, matted grass growing close to the ground.

It was native buffalo grass, more nutritious than any other kind. Heat and drought couldn't kill it; cold winters cured it into hay; the trampling of hooves couldn't destroy it. It was said this short grass could put two hundred extra pounds on a steer at maturity. A few minutes ago they had ridden through some ripening blue joint. Taller than the buffalo grass, its wheatlike heads had brushed the stirrups of his saddle.

The great herds of buffalo that had once roamed this range were well on their way to being exterminated by buffalo hunters and hiders. It was an act encouraged by the government in Washington in a deliberate attempt to break the spirit of the Plains Indians and subdue them once and for all. A year before, on October 5, 1877, Chief Joseph of the Nez Percé had surrendered over in the Bear Paw Mountains. Most of the Sioux and the Cheyenne were corraled on reservations, and the rest had fled to Canada with Sitting Bull and Dull Knife. After years of pressure from clamoring ranchers and railroads, the government was finally throwing open the last isolated island of open range. All this land was going to be free for the taking.

Chase Benteen Calder scanned the limitless expanse of the plains with sharp and knowing eyes. His glance stopped on the wiry rider sitting loosely on his horse. Both men were seasoned veterans of a half-dozen trail drives of longhorns north to the railheads in Kansas and beyond. They had just come off a drive Benteen had bossed for the Ten Bar ranch south of Fort Worth, Texas, to deliver a herd to an outfit in the Wyoming Territory. The horses they were riding and the ones that carried their packs all had the 10-brand burned on their hips.

It was on the trail during a stopover at Dodge City that they'd heard the first talk about the Indian country of Montana Territory and Benteen's interest had been aroused. Then, the ramrod of the Wyoming outfit had mentioned the free grass opening up to the north. Instead of heading directly back to Texas, Benteen had taken this side trip to get a look at the country, and Barnie had tagged along.

This vast rolling grassland was all that they had claimed it to be, and more. Its lower altitude made it more desirable than the plains of Wyoming and Colorado, and its grasses were rich—capable of putting hard weight on cattle.

There would be a stampede into the territory. Free grass was like whispering "gold." Right now, it looked like a sea of gold. Summer had ripened it to a rich yellow and autumn's cool breath was bronzing the heavy-headed grasses that covered hundreds of square miles. Its location wouldn't stay a secret for long. Soon the place would be overrun with people arriving to make their big chance. Would-be ranchers and speculators would come crawling out of the woodwork like cockroaches to try to make a quick buck and run. But Benteen made up his mind to be here before the cockroaches came.

"I think this is it, Barnie." His narrow smile was cool and sure.

"Yep." Barnabas Moore didn't need an explanation of that statement.

Three things were required to make a good cattle range—grass, water, and natural shelter from winter storms. There was grass aplenty; plum thickets and chokecherry trees offered brush shelter; and just ahead there was the wide course of a riverbed meandering through the heaving plains.

Looping the reins around the horse's neck, Benteen swung into the saddle and turned his mount and packhorse toward the cottonwood-lined banks of the river. The taciturn Barnie Moore followed, swaying loosely in rhythm to his horse's gait.

"Look there." Barnie nodded, the rolled front brim of his hat pointing to a cutbank where erosion by water and wind had exposed strata of rock and earth in the slope. Close to the surface, a wide seam of shiny black coal gleamed in the autumn sunlight. "Won't lack for fuel."

Surrounded by virtually treeless ridges, it was an important scrap of information to be tucked away for future use. Benteen made a mental note of it as both men continued toward the river without slacking their horses' pace.

Summer had reduced the river's flow to a sluggish current. It was well within the banks carved by spring melts, the shallow water running crystal clear. But it was water—life-giving, life-sustaining water.

Benteen let the reins sag on the saddlehorn. Beside him, Barnie reached into the deep pocket of his vest and fetched out his tobacco sack and paper. Certainty eased through Chase Benteen Calder. There was no longer any need to search this stark, lonely Montana land.

His eyes were filled with the enormous landscape, the sprawling plains valley with its shallow river flowing through it, the upthrust of range beyond it—and the high blue sky. This range reached from here to forever.

And it sang its promise to him. It sounded crazy to think the land was singing to him, but it was. The low murmur of the water set the rhythm while a keening breeze swept down the slope, playing a melody in the grasses and the dry leaves of the cottonwoods and willows bordering the river.

In his mind's eye, Benteen could see it all as it would be, herds of cattle growing fat on the native grasses, big barns walled with thick wood beams, and a big house sitting on that knoll from which he could view it all. Not in the beginning, but someday. In the meantime, there was plenty of room in these wide-open spaces to think and breathe and dream—and work like hell to make the dream a reality.

Benteen knew about work. He'd been working all his life for somebody else, but always watching and learning, putting aside money for a place of his own. All of it had been preparing him for this day when he rode onto this land where his knowledge and skill would be put to use. These trackless plains were going to carry his mark. Here he would build something that would endure.

The conviction that he'd found his home range swelled in his chest. This was his. This would be Calder land. "I'm filing on this stretch of river," he stated as Barnie licked his cigarette together.

Every cattleman knew that laying claim to a narrow stretch of the allowed 160-acre homestead tract gave control of an entire region—a minimum of ten miles on either side, or as far as a cow could walk to water. Elbow room increased it by at least another ten miles, and sometimes more. Barnie had already agreed that if Benteen found the right rangeland, he'd file on the adjoining stretch and turn it over to him, which was a common practice of the day. The additional 160 acres would give him breathing room—with more to come.

Texas had given Benteen his fill of being hemmed in and crowded. He'd been a boy at the close of the Civil War, but he'd seen the changes that had come with Reconstruction—few of them good. There had been too many lost causes in his young life. Here was the place for new beginnings.

"Come spring, I'll bring up a herd," Benteen stated in a spare, even tone while Barnie cupped a match to the hand-rolled cigarette and bent a little toward the flame. "If all goes well, I'll be back before the end of next summer. Do you think you can hang on here till then?"

"Reckon," Barnie drawled. He was younger by two years than Benteen. "What do you suppose yore pa'll do?"

Benteen looked into the distance, a net of crow-tracks springing from the outer corners of his eyes. "I don't know." The sun-browned skin became taut across the ridgeline of his jaw. "The Ten Bar's got him choked off the range. But he's a stubborn man."

His father, Seth Calder, was a good man—a strong man. It was possible he could have been an important man, but he had a blind spot, a fatal flaw. He didn't know when to let go of a thing that was dead. The War Between the States had ended years ago, yet his father continued to argue the South's cause, insisting Lincoln had thrown a political blanket over the true issue of states' rights that had prompted secession and turned the war into a question of slavery. That position hadn't made him popular with those in power in a Reconstructed Texas.

His support of the South during the war had left him nearly broke at its end. He struggled to rebuild his modest ranch, only to be wiped out by the Black Friday crash in the Panic of '73. Judd Boston's Ten Bar had survived the crash unscathed. While Seth Calder had to sell cattle, Judd Boston had purchased more, until Ten Bar herds flooded the range, leaving little room for Seth Calder to expand without overstocking the land. He was crowded into a small corner of ground that could barely support a cattle operation, but he wouldn't budge.

And Seth Calder wouldn't let go of the idea that his wife would come back to him. Benteen had spent most of his childhood waiting for a mother who never returned. She had chosen his name at birth—Chase Benteen Calder. Chase had been her maiden name, and Benteen the name of a cousin. His given name was rarely used by those who knew him. Even as a child, he'd been called Benteen.

When he was six years old, his mother had run away with a so-called remittance man—a ne'er-do-well paid a regular allowance by his moneyed English family to stay away from home. His father had always claimed that he'd lured her away with his talk of New Orleans, San Francisco, London, and Europe, of fancy gowns and jewels. After twenty years, Seth still believed she'd return to her husband and son. Benteen didn't. And, unlike his father, he didn't want her to come back.

There were times when a man should stand and fight—and other times when he should cut and run. Benteen saw that, but he doubted that his father would. In Texas, they were outnumbered by memories of the past and a series of present circumstances. Tomorrow was here in Montana Territory. "What about Lorna?" The closeness that had developed between them allowed Barnie to ask the personal question.

"We'll be married in the spring before the herd starts north." There was no more reason to wait. Benteen had found the place that would give them a future. And that was all that had been keeping him from setting a date for his wedding to Lorna Pearce. His gaze was sure and keen, a little on the reckless side. "The next time I leave Texas, it will be for good." He was going to cut all ties, and whatever was left behind . . . was left behind.

# Stands a Calder Man

# 1

AN INDIFFERENT SUN sat in the endless stretch of Montana sky, blazing down on the confused and bawling steers that jammed the cattle pens next to the railroad track. The chugging hiss of the motionless locomotive could barely be heard above the bewildered lowing of the steers and the clatter of cloven hooves on the wooden ramp of the loading chutes. The noise was punctuated by shouts and curses from cowboys as they poked the steers with long prods to force them up the chute and into the rail cars.

"Eighteen!"

With one cattle car filled to capacity, the locomotive rumbled out of its idle snoring to pull its string of cars ahead so the next one could be loaded. Plumes of smoke rose from its stack as the lumbering train's clanks and rattles added to the existing cacophony. Loading cattle destined for the slaughterhouses in the East was a tedious chore, made more unpleasant by the noise and the collective stench of penned animals.

Benteen Calder watched the proceedings from the sidelines. The wide hat brim shaded his suncreased features and partially concealed his restless, assessing gaze. His dark hair was shot with silver and the middle fifties had put some weight on his big-boned frame, but there was no mistaking that he was of the kind that produced the cattle kings. Piece by piece, he had carved out the Triple C Ranch with his sweat, his blood, and his cunning. He'd fought outlaws, renegade Indians, and greedy neighbors to keep the ranch. There would always be someone wanting it. And the man christened Chase Benteen Calder knew that.

The cattle being driven up the loading chute carried the Triple C brand, marking them as the property of the Calder Cattle Company—his ranch. The dry summer had left the steers in less than top condition for market, but the weather in eastern Montana was seldom ideal.

After nearly six weeks of roundup, Benteen was

conscious of the soreness in his aging muscles. Absently, he rubbed at the stiffness in his left arm. He picked up a movement to the right and shifted his head slightly to identify the figure approaching him. The corners of his mouth lifted in a silent greeting as Benteen recognized the railroad man, Bobby John Thomas.

"Oughta be through loadin' here in another hour," the man observed without any preliminary greeting.

"More or less," Benteen agreed with a faint nod.

The local railroad man's sharp eyes spotted a steer with an odd brand among the penned cattle. "I see you picked up some estrays. Diamond T." He read the brand and frowned. "Don't recall seeing that brand around here."

"I think it's a Dakota brand." It was impossible to know the various brands of ranches located outside of the state, and Benteen didn't try. "All told, we've got fourteen estrays in this shipment."

A description of each was listed on the shipping manifest. Given the wandering tendencies of cattle and their lack of respect for boundary lines or fences, it was inevitable that a beef roundup would include cattle owned by other outfits. Reps from neighboring ranches were always on hand for just that reason. If there was no representative for a given brand with the crew, the animal was always included in the market shipment. Left to roam, the estrayed cattle would eventually die of old age, benefiting no one. More important, it would eat grass that could have supported the range owner's cattle.

When the estrayed steer arrived at the terminal market, a brand inspector would spot it and payment for its sale would be forwarded to the animal's rightful owner. Such a practice, by both the rancher finding the estray and the brand inspector, was regarded as a courtesy of the range, observed by all and rarely abused. It was the Golden Rule put into practice—"Do unto others as you would have them do unto you."

Another railroad car had its load of steers and the door was slid shut. The train's engine began a racing chug to bring the next car into position. During the short respite in the loading operation, one of the cowboys stepped down from his perch on the chute and removed his hat, wiping his forearm across his brow, then jammed his hat back onto his nearly black hair all in one motion. A brief glimpse at his angular features, the color and texture of richly grained leather, was enough to hint at a similarity between the young cowboy and the owner of the penned cattle.

Bobby John Thomas looked at Benteen. "Is that yore boy Webb?"

There was an imperceptible tightening of Benteen's mouth as he nodded an affirmative answer. A troubled light flickered in his eyes, put there by a gnawing worry that wouldn't go away.

"He sure has growed since the last time I saw him," the railroad agent remarked.

"Yeah." The abruptness of the response seemed to carry a negative connotation. Benteen didn't volunteer the information that, so far, Webb had only grown in size. The promise his son had shown in his early years hadn't yet developed in adulthood.

There was much about the tall, huskily built youth for Benteen to be proud of. At twenty-six, Webb was one of the top hands on the Triple C Ranch. He could ride the rankest bronc, rope with the best of them, and turn his hand to almost anything. Webb never shirked from hard work, so Benteen couldn't fault him for that. It was responsibility that Webb avoided, accepting it only when it was forced on him. On those rare occasions, he handled it well, making few wrong decisions. But it was that lack of interest in assuming an active role in the management of the ranch that troubled Benteen. The more he pushed Webb about it, reminding him that the Triple C would be his someday, the less interest Webb displayed.

Lorna didn't help the situation by insisting that Benteen was expecting too much from their son. It was her opinion that Webb was still too young and needed time to sow his wild oats before taking on any responsibility in running the ranch. Maybe she was right, but he'd been the same age as Webb when he'd driven the herd of Longhorns north from Texas to found the Triple C Ranch. It worried him to think he'd raised a son who was content to take orders instead of giving them. The future of the ranch depended on his son.

Moving his attention from the leanly muscled frame of his big-boned son, the source of his vague anxiety, Benteen half-turned toward the agent. His face showed none of his inner disturbance.

"Ya been keeping busy, Bobby John?" he inquired.

"We've been busy, but we haven't been makin' much money," the agent declared on a rueful note.

Benteen's mouth quirked in a dry line. "That's always the railroad's complaint. And it gets harder to swallow every time I see the freight rates go up."

"It's a fact." Bobby John was a loyal company man. "We may haul a lot of cattle out of Miles City in the fall, but we don't haul enough in or out on a regular basis. We just ain't got the people here, or the goods."

"I suppose," Benteen conceded.

"That might all change, though." The comment was made, then left to lie there like a baited hook allowed to settle near a submerged log where a big fish rested.

Benteen's interest in the conversation was no longer idle, his curiosity aroused by the remark. "Why is that?"

"Some fella plowed him some ground up around the Musselshell River and planted him some wheat. Rumor has it that he harvested forty bushels to an acre." He saw the skepticism in Benteen's dark eyes. "He used that dryland method of farming like they developed in Kansas."

Benteen had a sketchy understanding of the principle involved in such a method. In arid land where there wasn't a local water source to provide irrigation, crops were planted on only half the acreage while the other half was left fallow. This idle land was plowed and harrowed so no plant life would consume any moisture that fell on it. The next year, that half would be planted to crops. It was a way of conserving the moisture from rain and snow for the next year's use.

"It won't work here," Benteen stated flatly,

regardless of the evidence just given to the contrary. "This is cow country. That's all it is good for. Besides, I've never heard of a farmer yet who could make a living on just eighty acres." That was half of the one hundred and sixty acres entitled for home- stead, and the only part that was productive at any one time under the dryland method of farming.

"That may be true," Bobby John admitted. "But I've heard talk that there's a proposal bein' pre- sented to the Congress to double the amount of acreage allowed under the Homestead Act."

Benteen's chin lifted a fraction of an inch in reaction to this new information. An uneasy feeling ran through him as he looked beyond the cattle pens of the railroad yard to the grassland.

In the autumn afternoon the stark Montana landscape looked like a sea of tanned stalks. It was the best damned grass any cowman could hope to find. The idea of its being ripped up by a plow and replaced by wheat was more than he could stand. A lot of things were different from the way they had been when he had first arrived in the territory, but this was one change Benteen wouldn't accept. He'd fight any attempt to turn this cow country into farmland.

"They'll never be able to push that bill through Congress." There was a steely quality to his voice, but the prospect of a battle, political or otherwise, added its weight to the tiredness in his bones.

"I wouldn't be too sure about that," Bobby John Thomas warned him. "It ain't just a bunch of land-hungry farmers that wants to see it pass." But he added no more than that.

Benteen silently cursed himself for speaking without thinking through the opposition. Farmers were the least of his worries. It was the railroads. They were land-poor in this part of the West, owners of thousands of square-mile tracts of land along their right-of-way, deeded to them by the U.S. government for laying track. The railroads would use an enlarged Homestead Act like a carrot to lure the farmers out here and end up selling them land for farms or townsites. They'd create a land boom that would bring settlers in, tradesmen as well as farmers. People needed products, which meant more freight generated for the railroads.

It didn't take much intelligence to figure it out. The railroads had done the same thing in Kansas, Nebraska, and Colorado, where that prairie sod was now sown with some Russian strain of wheat. But this land wasn't the same. Methods that worked there couldn't work here.

The proposal coming before Congress had to be stopped, and stopped swiftly. Benteen knew in his gut that he couldn't waste any time, yet the six-week-long roundup had left him in a state of fatigue. Even if he looked the physical equal of his son, he no longer had the resilience of his youth.

"Guess I'd better be gettin' back to my office." Bobby John Thomas shifted his position in a show of reluctance to put his words into action, but Benteen said nothing to invite the railroad agent to stay longer and chat. "Give my regards to your missus."

"I will." An image formed in his mind of Lorna waiting for him at the hotel in town. He suddenly felt an overwhelming need to be with her. Benteen barely noticed the agent move away, his attention already traveling down another channel. His glance swept the cattle pens and loading platform in an effort to locate Barnie Moore, then came to a stop on his son. Dammit, it was going to be his ranch and his land someday, Benteen thought with a frown of irritable concern. "Webb!" There was an edge to his voice as he raised its volume to make himself heard.

With a turn of his head, Webb looked over his shoulder and saw the single motion from his father that indicated he wanted to speak to him. He swung down from the loading chute onto the platform and handed the long prod to another cowboy to take his place. As Webb approached his father, he experienced that strange feeling of pride and resentment—pride for the man that Chase Benteen Calder was and the wide swath he'd cut across this land practically single-handedly, and resentment for the same reasons.

He didn't want to be his father's son; he didn't want to be singled out from the other hands because his name was Calder; he wanted to earn his right to command, even though he was born in the position to inherit it. He would rather have been born Webb Smith than Webb Calder, so his was a quiet rebellion—never overt, always subtle—denying himself the right to claim what was his by birth. Webb made it a practice not to assert himself or his opinions with the other ranch hands. In spite of that, all the cowboys, except the older ones who had come north with his father, turned to Webb whenever there was a decision to be made, deferring to him because he was a Calder. That angered him, although he seldom let it show.

Webb knew his father was disappointed in him. He'd been lectured enough times about accepting responsibility. Only once had Webb tried to explain the way he felt, his determination to be accepted because of his ability, rather than rest on the circumstances of his birth. His father had brushed it aside as a foolish whim, needlessly reminding Webb that he couldn't change the fact that he was born a Calder. Rebuffed by this lack of understanding, Webb had taken the lonely path, not able to be just one of the boys and refusing to assume the role his father wanted for him. More than once, he had considered tying his bedroll on the back of his saddle and riding away from the Triple C; then he'd think about his mother and he'd stay, hoping something would change.

"Yes, sir?" Webb stopped in front of his father, letting the inflection of his voice question why he had been summoned. He hadn't addressed him as Pa in more than six years.

There was nothing in his son's attitude or expression that showed more than casual interest. Benteen probed, hoping to find more. He never knew what the boy was thinking—or if he was thinking. A father should know what was going on in his son's head. Benteen knew he didn't.

"I want you to go to the telegraph office and send some wires for me," Benteen stated. "One of them goes to Frank Bulfert, the senator's aide, in Washington. In the wire, I want you to ask him the status of the proposal being brought to Congress to enlarge the Homestead Act and what kind of preliminary support it's getting. Ask for the same information from Asa Morgan in Helena. The last wire I want you to send to Bull Giles at the Black Dove Bar in Washington with the same request for information." The lack of interest Webb showed made him feel weary. "Have you got all that?"

"Yes, sir." Behind the smooth exterior, his mind was running over the possible significance of the information being sought and how it might affect the ranch. "Is there anything else?"

"No." His lips thinned into a tired line. "Don't you want to know why this information is important?" Benteen asked, and had the satisfaction of seeing his son's steady gaze waver briefly.

"I figured you'd tell me when you thought it was right for me to know." There was no hesitation over the reply, and the invitation to ask the question wasn't accepted.

Frustrated by his son's behavior, Benteen half-turned from him, muttering, "Go send the wires, and have the replies directed to the hotel."

As Webb moved away, spurs rattling with each stride, the aching numbness returned in Benteen's left shoulder and arm. He rubbed at the soreness, kneading the muscles with his fingers.

"What's the matter with your arm?" The voice asking the question belonged to Barnie Moore.

Benteen let his right hand slide down the arm

and shrugged aside the nagging ache. "Too many nights sleeping on cold, hard ground, I guess."

"I know what 'cha mean." Barnie arched his back, as if flexing stiff muscles. "Neither one of us is as young as we used to be." His gaze followed Webb. "I remember when that one was just a pup, playin' around with my boy. Now both of them is full-growed men."

Benteen sighed irritably. "I wish I knew where I went wrong with him."

"Webb?" Barnie frowned at him. "There isn't a better cowboy on the ranch than him."

"It isn't a cowboy I want," Benteen replied, but didn't confide the doubts he had about Webb's ability to become the ranch's leader. "How many more carloads of steers do we have left?"

Barnie took the cue to change the subject. "About eight or nine, I'd say." When he noticed the haggard lines etched in Benteen's features, he concealed his concern by casually rolling a smoke. "No need for you to stick around. We can handle the rest."

Benteen hesitated, but the constant din at the railroad pens grated on nerves that were already raw. "I'll be at the hotel if you need me."

Barnie nodded acknowledgment, although he didn't look up as he tapped tobacco from the pouch onto the trough of cigarette paper.

When Benteen stopped at the hotel desk to pick up the key to the suite, there was a message waiting for him. "Your wife said to tell you she'd gone shopping, Mr. Calder," the clerk informed him.

Annoyance flickered across his expression as he closed his fingers around the key and clipped out an automatic "Thank you."

"Be sure to let us know if there's anything you need," the clerk offered, not wanting the hotel to be responsible for the displeasure of a guest as important as Benteen Calder.

"Have someone bring up a bottle of your best whiskey," he ordered.

A quick smile spread across the clerk's face. "Your wife has already seen to that, sir. It's waiting in your room."

As he climbed the stairs to the suite, Benteen made a silent wager with himself that there would be a fresh cigar waiting for him in addition to the bonded whiskey. He won the bet. It was his wife's thoughtfulness that softened the hard curves of his mouth more than the cigar and the sipping whiskey. Shrugging out of his jacket, he dropped it and his hat on a chair in the suite's sitting room and sat down in the second chair, stretching out his legs full length in front of him.

Although the whiskey he'd splashed in the glass

was barely touched, the cigar was half-smoked when Benteen heard the soft laughter of female voices in the hotel corridor. A key was turned in the lock and the door was pushed inward. His instinct was to stand, but a lethargy seemed to have control of his muscles as Lorna swept into the room with a rustle of skirt and petticoats.

Her arms were laden with packages. The young, blond-haired girl who followed her into the suite was similarly burdened. Benteen couldn't help noticing that Lorna didn't look that much older than the teenaged girl. She claimed there were gray strands in her dark hair, but they were so few that they didn't show. Her figure retained its slim, youthful curves and her complexion was china-smooth, showing only fine hairline cracks of age—thanks to the lotions she used to combat the effects of Montana's harsh climate. No one looking at her would guess at her inner strength, or the hardships she'd suffered in the early years. Her struggle to come to grips with this land had been as great as his own. With Lorna at his side, Benteen felt there was nothing he couldn't handle.

"I hope Daddy won't think I spent too much," young Ruth Stanton declared with a trace of apprehension.

Neither woman had noticed Benteen yet. He

didn't mind. He liked the opportunity to watch Lorna unobserved. After setting her packages on the table just inside the room, she was unpinning the feathered blue silk hat.

"Your father wanted you to buy nice things for yourself," Lorna insisted, still addressing the daughter of her late friend. Since pneumonia had claimed Mary Stanton's life last winter, she had taken Ruth under her wing. Benteen suspected it filled a void in both lives, easing their grief. As a surrogate mother to Ruth, Lorna had acquired the daughter she had always longed for, while Ruth had an older woman to act as adviser and role model.

Ash was building on the end of his cigar. Benteen tapped it off. It was either his movement or the smell of cigar smoke, or both, that suddenly attracted Lorna's attention to the side of the room where he was sitting.

"Benteen." Lorna set the blue hat atop the packages as she crossed the room to greet him, her dark eyes radiant with delight. "No one at the desk mentioned you were here. Why didn't you say something when we came in?" Bending, she brushed her lips against the roughness of his cheek, then straightened, letting her hand rest on his shoulder to maintain contact.

"I knew you'd notice me sitting here sooner or

later." A smile touched the corners of his mouth. "It looks like the two of you bought out the town."

"We tried." Lorna winked at Ruth in mock conspiracy.

An attractive girl with curling blond hair and quiet blue eyes, Ruth Stanton was innately shy. Even though Benteen had been the closest thing to an uncle all her life, she wasn't able to directly meet his gaze. Her glance skipped quickly back to Lorna.

"I'd better take these packages to my room." She almost pounced on the excuse to leave.

"We'll meet you in the dining room at six." Lorna didn't attempt to detain the girl. "Webb will be there, too. Why don't you wear your new pink dress?"

"Yes, I will." The suggestion brought a flush of pleasure to Ruth's cheeks. With a circumspect nod to Benteen, she slipped out the door to cross the hallway to her room.

When they were alone, Benteen tipped his head back to eye his wife. "Are you sure Webb's joining us for dinner?" With the roundup over and the cattle on their way to market, most of the Triple C riders would be doing the town. And Webb counted himself among them.

"He'll be there if I have to drag him out of the

saloon myself," Lorna stated with a determined gleam in her eyes.

His mouth crooked in a wry line. "Maybe it won't be a saloon he's in," he suggested dryly.

"It won't make any difference." She moved away from his chair, recrossing the room to the table with the packages. "Do you mind if I ask you something?" She sounded too casual.

"What?" Benteen was instantly alert, prepared for almost anything.

"Is it true that Connie the Cowboy Queen had a dress embroidered with the brand of every outfit from here to the Platte?" When Lorna turned to look at him, there was a beguiling innocence about her expression that made Benteen shake his head.

"Where do you hear about these things?" Even after all these years, she still managed to surprise him now and again. Connie the Cowboy Queen had been one of the more notorious prostitutes in Miles City in its heyday.

"Women do talk about things other than sewing, cooking, and children. I promise that I looked properly shocked," she assured him with a mocking glance. "Was the Triple C brand embroidered on her dress, Benteen?"

"How should I know?" Amusement glinted in his eyes.

But she wasn't buying his attempt at ignorance. "A man can frequent such establishments without sampling the wares. Or maybe you just never saw her with a dress on?" Lorna pretended to accuse him of infidelity.

"When I had more woman than I could handle at home?" Benteen countered with a lift of one eyebrow; then it straightened to its natural line. "As for the dress, there was such a thing. And it wouldn't have been complete without the Triple C brand on it." His gaze narrowed on her with wary censure. "I hope this isn't the sort of thing you tell Ruth. The poor girl probably hasn't been kissed yet."

"No, I haven't gotten around to discussing any intimate topics with her." The implication was that the day was coming when Lorna would. Turning sideways to keep Benteen within her vision, she began untying the strings around the packages. "I'm certain Ruth is more than a little in love with Webb."

"Is that why you're going to make sure he comes to dinner tonight—and why Ruth is going to wear her new pink dress?"

Lorna paused to gaze wistfully into space. "Wouldn't it be wonderful if our son and Mary's daughter eventually married?" She barely controlled a sigh as she resumed the opening of her parcels. "It seems only fitting to me."

"I wouldn't hold out much hope." Benteen bolted down the half-jigger of whiskey in his glass in an effort to burn out the sour taste in his mouth. "You'll probably have about as much success trying to marry Webb off to Ruth as I've had trying to turn him into a rancher—which is zero."

"You're too impatient." Lorna gave him a mildly critical look. "You grew up in a different time, under different circumstances, so you can't judge Webb by your life."

The glass was abruptly set on the table next to the chair as Benteen pulled his feet under him and pushed upright. "Maybe that's the problem," he declared grimly. "I haven't been hard enough on him. I've let you spoil him."

"Me?" She stiffened at the challenging statement.

But Benteen was following the thought through aloud while he prowled restlessly around the sitting room. "Everything's been handed to him since the day he was born. He's been fussed over, coddled— the center of attention. Everyone's always smoothing the way for him. He's never had to fight for anything in his life."

"That isn't true." Lorna's maternal instinct rose

with a rush as she confronted Benteen and forced him to stop his pacing. "Just look at how hard Webb has worked to earn the respect of the other riders. He's never let them treat him any differently because he's the boss's son."

"Why doesn't he work that hard to earn *my* respect?" Benteen insisted, his dark brows puckering together in a wistful line. "I can buy a dozen cowboys as good as Webb is at working cattle for thirty dollars a month and found. I don't need another workhorse in harness; I need someone who can hold the reins."

"Give him time," Lorna argued.

"There isn't that much left." He sighed and turned away from her. Defeat was tugging at his shoulders, but he kept them squared. "He doesn't give a damn about the ranch." He was beginning to believe that.

"Yes, he does." Her voice was steady, firm in its conviction. "It's his home."

"I'll take your word for it." He wished he hadn't brought up the subject. Long, stiff strides carried him to the table, where he crushed out the cigar. "I'd better shave and get washed up for dinner."

Before he'd taken two steps toward the adjoining bedroom, there was a knock at the door. He paused, waiting to find out who was outside, while Lorna walked to the door, the exaggerated bustle of her dress wig-wagging huffy signals at him.

"Hello, Mother," Webb greeted her as the door swung inward. A gentleness softened the hard edges of his raw-boned features, giving them a warmth of expression they usually lacked.

"Webb." For an instant, Lorna faltered in surprise and sent a darting glance over her shoulder at Benteen, hoping Webb's arrival on the heels of their discussion wouldn't precipitate a second and, perhaps, angry one. She didn't like being caught in the middle, her loyalties divided between husband and son.

The case went out of Webb's expression as his gaze traveled past her to his father. The atmosphere seemed thick with tension, strong undercurrents running between his parents.

"Come in, Webb," his father stated in a voice that sounded grimly resigned. "Your mother and I were just talking about you."

When his mother's glance faltered under his silent inspection and she moved out of the doorway to admit him, Webb stepped into the room. Obviously he'd been the subject of disagreement between them. He didn't want to be the cause of disharmony for his parents. He just wanted to live life his way, on his terms.

"Yes, we were," his mother agreed with commendable aplomb. "I was just threatening to drag you out of whatever saloon or bawdy house you were in so we could all have dinner together tonight. Now that you're here, your father can be spared that embarrassment."

"I came by"—Webb paused to direct his explanation to his father—"to let you know that all the wires have been sent. The replies will be coming to you here."

"Wires?" Lorna sent a questioning look at Benteen, mildly curious because it seemed a less quarrelsome topic, and because he hadn't mentioned telegraphing anyone. "What's this all about?"

"Nothing that needs to concern you."

"Someday I hope you'll explain to me why you always insist something is none of my business when other people are around, and then tell me about it later when we are alone," she lightly taunted him. "Men seem to think the only place they can talk to their wives is in the bedroom. But it isn't true, Webb," she advised her son.

The corners of his mouth deepened with a hidden smile at his mother's daring. Webb noticed his father was wavering between irritation and amusement.

"I'll try to remember," Webb murmured dryly.

"I thought I married a quiet, tractable woman." Benteen shook his head in affectionate exasperation. "I hope you have better luck, son."

"That reminds me," Lorna inserted. "We'll meet you at six this evening in the dining room." She ran a mother's critical eye over his dusty, smelly clothes and beard-roughened face. "That will give you time to bathe and change clothes. Ruth came to town with me to do some shopping, so she'll be joining us for dinner, too."

The last bit of information left Webb feeling a little unsettled without knowing why. He liked Ruth. She was practically family—a younger sister.

Yet his mother had been quite insistent about him cleaning up and changing clothes. Surely a man didn't have to make a special point about that for a girl who was like a sister. Unless his mother didn't want him to regard Ruth as a sister. A glint of amusement appeared in his eyes at her subtle maneuvering.

"It was good of you to bring her to town, Mother," he commented. "I know it hasn't been easy for her since Mary passed away. She needed to get out and away from the house."

"That's what I thought," his mother agreed with a pleased smile.

"I'd better get cleaned up." Webb started to turn toward the door to leave.

"Oh, Webb—" She called him back, faltering for a second. "Be sure to notice the dress she's wearing tonight. It's a new one."

"I will." He was smiling as he left the suite. A compliment was expected to be issued about the new gown. It didn't seem to matter how old he got; his mother still felt obligated to remind him about his manners and gentlemanly behavior. Or was it another attempt to arouse a more personal interest in the woman wearing the new dress?

Lorna closed the door and leaned against it, chewing thoughtfully on the inside of her lower lip. When she became aware of Benteen watching her, she straightened. "While you're washing up, I think I'll help Ruth fix her hair."

"Matchmaking is like leading a horse to water. You can't make him drink," Benteen cautioned.

"No, but maybe he'll remember where the water is and find it again himself when he's thirsty," Lorna reasoned. She wasn't sure if it was the fading afternoon light or whether she simply hadn't looked at him so closely before, but Benteen suddenly looked tired to her. "Maybe you should lie down and rest a bit before dinner."

"I'm fine." An impatient frown deepened the

lines already carved in his face. He started once again for the bedroom and stopped. "The last address we had on Bull Giles after he left Denver—was it the Black Dove in Washington?"

"Yes." It was her turn to frown.

"That's what I thought." He nodded absently.

"Did you have Webb send a wire to him?" She had already guessed the answer was affirmative. "Why?"

"He may have dropped out of the political scene, but he's bound to have some connections yet. There's a bill coming before Congress that has got to be stopped," Benteen explained vaguely. "It would throw this whole state open to homesteaders and plows. I don't want to go into it just now, not until I find out the particulars."

"That's what's been troubling you, isn't it?"

"Partly." He rubbed a hand along the side of his neck. "And I'm tired. Tired of struggling to keep what we've got. It wouldn't be so bad if my son was fighting with me. It's battling alone—"

"You're not alone." She glided quickly across the space that separated them and curved her hands around his forearm, tipping her head back to look at him.

"No, I'm not alone," Benteen agreed, but there was a sad light in his brown eyes. "I don't really mind the fight. But I'm not getting any younger. What happens when I'm gone, Lorna? I worry about you and how you'll manage on your own. I can't depend on Webb to look out for you anymore."

She caught her breath on a rising note of fear. "You're just tired, Benteen." She made a desperate attempt to dismiss his remarks as exaggerations. "Things will look better after you've rested a couple of days."

"Yeah." But he didn't sound convinced as he patted her hand and moved away toward the bedroom.

# This Calder Sky

# 1

BENEATH A CLEAR SKY, the Montana plains rolled to the far horizon in an undulating sea of grass. This great, sprawling rangeland was broken by lonely buttes and wandering ravines. It was a huge, almost empty, always challenging land. Its vastness made the small man smaller and the big man king.

Where once the shaggy-maned buffalo had grazed, a herd of six hundred red-coated Hereford cattle was gathered in a pocket of the plains. Held in place by an encircling group of riders, they bawled their discontent. Into this milling confusion, cowboys working in pairs walked their horses into the herd to slowly and methodically cut out the crippled cattle—dry cows, the cows with poor spring calves, and the odd steer that had escaped the previous autumn's roundup.

Webb Calder pointed the nose of his claybank stud at the cow to be separated from the herd, then sat deep and easy in the saddle to let the horse do its work. The stallion was the color of the yellow mountain cat from which it took its name, Cougar. The instant the cow was isolated, the claybank frustrated its every attempt to rejoin the herd—getting low, coming around on a dime, and springing forward with the swiftness of a cat.

To the big-boned man in the saddle, the rangy stallion was a source of pride. He'd picked the horse out of a range-wild group of yearlings and earmarked it for his personal remuda. The breaking and training he'd done himself, turning the animal into the best cow horse on the spread. It was never something Webb Calder bragged about, and any compliment was met with the casually indifferent reply, "The claybank is good."

He had a philosophy that if you were the best, you didn't have to tell anybody—and if you weren't, then you'd damned well better keep your mouth shut. He lived by it, and expected the others around him to live by it, too.

When he and the yellow horse had the cow separated from the herd, the cowboys moved in from the flanks to push the animal over the lip of the ground's pocket to where the cut of injured or inferior cattle were being held. Two more riders took his place to work the herd.

Riding back to the gather, Webb was joined by Nate Moore, who had worked the cut with him. The lank, weatherbeaten rider was one of a small corps of cowboys who had their roots dug as deep into this Montana range as Webb Calder had. Yet, some invisible quality stamped Webb Calder as the cattle owner.

For this was Calder land as far to the south as the eye could see, and beyond. All the livestock, except strays from the bordering small ranches to the north, carried the Triple C brand of the Calder Cattle Company. It was the heritage left by the first Calder who pulled up stakes in Texas and drove his herd north in 1878 to find free grass. That ancestor, Chase Benteen Calder, had carved out an empire that was measured in square miles numbering nearly six hundred. He'd held it against warring bands of renegade Indians, homesteaders, and jealously ambitious neighboring ranchers. He'd paid for it with Calder blood, nourished it with his sweat and the bones of drought-stricken cattle, and buried the Calder dead under the Montana grass.

Of the score of cowboys who had made the drive

with Chase Benteen Calder, most had drifted, but a few had stayed to build a new life in this raw land. These men formed the nucleus of the group of fore-runners to Nate Moore, Virg Haskell's wife, Ruth, Slim Trumbo, Ike Willis, and a handful of others, born and raised on the Calder ranch, like Webb. Their loyalty was a deep-seeded thing, ingrained into their souls as surely as if they carried the Triple C brand.

This thread of continuity ran through each gen-eration, tying them together. The old ones eventu-ally gave way to young blood, bringing change without ever changing.

Cresting the rise of the untamed plain, Webb reined in his horse. Satisfaction ran easy through him as he surveyed the scene before him, the team-work of all the riders working the herd with effi-cient, well-oiled precision. He liked it best when he could get out among them. Although he was there out of necessity, since his decision determined which was the poorer stock to be culled from this herd, the sheer pleasure of the work made him take part in the actual cutting of the cattle.

The pressures and responsibilities were enormous and endless for the man who owned a ranch as vast as this. New salesmen or cattle buyers often com-mented on its size, and Webb was fond of quipping dryly, "It takes a big chunk of ground to fit under a Calder sky." He didn't know how it ranked against other big ranches in the country, whether it was first, second, third, or far down on the list. If anyone asked him, he couldn't have answered and he didn't care enough to check. His only interests lay in making it prosper and keeping it intact for his son.

The responsibilities were heavy, but so was the power he wielded. Webb Calder believed himself to be a fair man. There were some who would say he was exacting. And still others would claim that he ruled with an iron hand. Resentment born out of envy and jealousy made him the object of hatred from a silent few. As far as Webb Calder was concerned, he had never raised his hand against a man without cause. When he acted, it was swift and with purpose. Indecision could eventually spell disaster for an outfit the size of the Triple C.

It was one of the things he'd tried to teach his son, Chase Calder, named after their Texan ancestor. There was more to running a ranch than keeping books, raising cattle, and going to the bank. But how do you teach a man to be a leader, to handle men?

Before Chase had taken his first step, Webb had set the baby boy on a saddle atop an old bellmare and wrapped the tiny fists around the saddle horn to take him on his first ride. By the time Chase was two, he was given the reins. When he was five, he went on his first roundup, tied to the saddle so he wouldn't fall off if he fell asleep.

Horses and cattle were part of living. Those things Chase learned by osmosis, unconsciously absorbing the knowledge into his system until it was second nature.

But it was the subtleties of command that Webb wanted him to learn. From the time the boy had understood his first sentence, Webb had tried to drum these things into his head, shaping and molding Chase to take over the ranch someday. He'd warned Chase that as his son, he would have to work longer, be smarter, and fight rougher than any man-jack out there. No favor would ever be granted him by Webb—no concession would ever be made because Chase was a Calder. There would be no special privileges because he was the rancher's son. In fact, the reverse would be true. In his teens, Chase had the hardest jobs, the rankest horses, and the longest hours of any man on the place. Any problems were his to solve. If there was trouble, he had to be man enough to fight his way out of it, either with his fists or his wits. Chase couldn't come to his father and expect help. Webb pushed him as hard as he dared without breaking the boy's spirit.

Even as Webb Calder watched the two dozen horsemen at work, he unconsciously and instinctively kept an eye on his son. Chase was taller than the average cowboy, wide in the shoulders and solid in the chest, yet youthfully lean and supple with a rider's looseness about him. The sun had burned a layer of tan over hard and angular Calder features. Dark-haired and dark-eyed, he seemed older than twenty-two—except when he smiled. Then he seemed careless and guileless. His son was still an unknown quantity to Webb. Maybe some might think he demanded too much, but he was firmly convinced it was the tough things that were good for a man.

The horse beside the claybank blew out a relaxed snort, making Webb shift his glance to Nate Moore. He was building a smoke and licked the paper with a stingy tongue. Without looking up, he spoke. "He's a good boy." He guessed the object of Webb's thoughts.

"Lil would be proud of him." Webb uttered his late wife's name and broke a silence that had lasted more than twenty years since her death. Time had erased the grief of his loss. Now the memory of her was another tradition.

It was something an outsider couldn't understand—this lack of expression the true Western man showed when he lost a comrade or a loved one—the failure to reveal keen sorrow. What a man felt was kept inside. The face an outsider saw looked cold and unemotional. Yet beneath the hard exteriors of these men, there was all the delicate sensitivity of a woman, hidden from view. Revealing it displayed weakness. This was a land where only the strong survived.

"Yes, she would," Nate spoke with the cigarette in his mouth and squinted his eyes at the pungent smoke curling from it. The expression deepened the sun-creased lines splaying from the corners of his eyes. Without turning his head, his attention shifted to the young cowboy, Buck Haskell, riding on the same side of the herd where Chase was. For apparently no reason, Buck had spun his sorrel horse to face the opposite direction and spurred it toward a slight gap between riders, reaching an invisible point the instant a cow attempted to break from the herd. Respect glinted in the older cowhand's eyes. "That Buckie has more cow sense than some cowboys three times his age," Nate declared. "And how he loves those rank broncs. The more contrary they are, the better he likes 'em."

Webb's mouth tightened. "Yeah, and he's always got his rope down. I've never caught him at it, but I know he does."

"Hell!" Nate chuckled. "Every young cowboy is going to sneak off and rope something now and then."

Webb conceded that with a lift of his heavy brows. "Buck is a likable boy, but I worry about that wild streak in him."

With curly blond hair, blue eyes, and a perpetual grin, Buck was Virg and Ruth Haskell's son, born two days before Chase. When Webb's wife, Lillian, didn't have enough milk to breast-feed Chase, Ruth had taken over as wet-nurse. A year and a half later, after Lil had died, Ruth cooked and kept house for Webb. So Buck and Chase had been raised practically as brothers. It was natural that Webb took extra interest in Buck.

The hand-rolled cigarette never left Nate's mouth, but he managed to pull the corners into a dry smile. "You're forgettin', Webb. We were wilder than that when we were twenty-two."

He exchanged a wry glance with the cowboy. "Maybe so."

From the broken land to the north, a trio of riders approached the herd's gathering point. Webb centered his gaze on the short, wiry rider a half-stride in the lead. His face lost its expression, becoming heavy-boned and hard.

"Who's that with O'Rourke?" He didn't take his eyes from the owner of the small, two-bit spread on a north strip of the Calder boundary.

Nate looked, his eyes narrowing less from the smoke and more from recognition. "His boy. The skinny one must be his girl." He had pulled the warmth from his voice, making it flat.

As he skimmed the pair riding with Angus O'Rourke, Webb inspected first the gangling eighteen-year-old boy with lank black hair sticking out from beneath his hat. The boy kept looking at his father, seeking some form of guidance. The girl was a small slip of a thing, looking more like a young boy than a girl. There was a glimpse of the slick, black sides of her hair beneath the hat, but Webb couldn't tell whether it was cut that short or pushed under the crown. Both the shirt and the Levi's appeared to be cast-offs of her brother's. Both were too large, making her look all the more skinny and shapeless. Except for the heavy fringe of lashes around her green eyes, there was nothing about the set of her features to distinguish her from an immature boy. There were spurs on the heels of her rundown boots, an old and cracked pair of leather gloves on her hands, and an ill-fitting jacket dwarfing her small frame. The sight of her rankled Webb.

"A girl shouldn't be doing a man's work," he muttered and turned his head to thrust his hard gaze at Nate. "You ride down there and tell the men to watch their language. If I hear so much as a 'goddamn' out of them with that girl around, there's going to be hell to pay when she leaves."

Nate pinched the fire off the end of his cigarette, letting the ember fall into the cuff of his denims, where it was crushed dead. The unsmoked portion of the cigarette was tucked away in his pocket as he reined his mount toward the cowboys working the herd.

Webb watched him leave. The modern world may have advanced into the space age with computers and high technology, but there were sections of the West where time had changed very little. Everything was more mechanized, but most of the work was still done on horseback.

The old codes lingered. Women were scarce and treated with respect until they showed they didn't deserve it. A man settled his own problems; he didn't take them to someone else. It wasn't hard to understand when put in perspective. In the case of the Triple C, there was a thirty-five-mile-long driveway before you reached the front porch of the main house. A respectable-sized town of more than a population of one hundred could be a hundred miles away, and more.

The Calder ranch sat on an area of land larger than the state of Rhode Island. With the kind of power that gave Webb Calder, he was virtually his own law, answerable to almost no one but God Almighty. Wisely, he never tried to ride roughshod over anyone else, only now and then letting his authority be felt. He turned a blind eye to the dirt-farming Andersen family trying to eke out a living on a half-section of ground on his east boundary. Webb knew they butchered a steer or two of his each year, but he wouldn't see women and children go hungry. But God help the man who lifted his hand against the Triple C for his own gain.

His gaze narrowed in silent speculation on Angus O'Rourke, who was riding toward him. The man spent too much time dreaming and found too many excuses for why he couldn't succeed. O'Rourke was a weak man, always wanting the easy way. There wasn't any place for that kind in this country. Sooner or later they were weeded out.

The hard, fixed stare from Calder made Angus uncomfortable. How he'd love to ride up and spit in the man's eye. He licked his dry lips nervously, telling himself that the day would come when he wouldn't have to kowtow to the likes of Webb Calder. But the assurance was old and rang hollow in his mind. He'd been a dark, handsome man once, with glib Irish charm, but lines of dissipation were beginning to take away his looks, and people no longer believed in his grandiose plans for the future, having heard too many in the past that came to naught.

"If he asks us anything, what should we say?" The anxiously whispered question came from his son.

Angus didn't turn his head or look around to answer. "Don't say anything. I'll do the talking."

"I told you we should have hazed those thirty head back across the fence last week, Pa," the girl stated calmly.

"And I told you they needed a few more days of good grass, Maggie!" The argument had already been hashed over several times. "Those cows just strayed, that's all. And we're just here to cut out our strays, like we always do."

He reined his horse down to a walk to cross the last few yards to Webb Calder, stopping at a right angle to him. Flashing the man one of his patented smiles, he respectfully touched a finger to the pointed brim of his Stetson.

"Good morning, Mr. Calder." Angus O'Rourke sounded deliberately cheerful and carefree.

"Angus." The stone-faced man with the hard eyes simply nodded in response to the greeting.

Irritation rippled through Angus. He was angry with himself for not calling Calder by his first name, and putting them on equal terms. The man had a way of making him feel worthless and a failure. Hell, he was a rancher, too, the same as Calder . . . in his mind. But Angus hid his bitterness well.

"It's a fine day, isn't it?" he remarked with a broad, encompassing sweep of the clear sky. "It's mornings like this that make you forget the long winter behind you. The meadowlarks out there singing away. Wildflowers are sprouting up all over, and those little white-faced calves all shiny and new." It was a few seconds before he realized his prattle was making no impression on Webb Calder. Again, Angus checked his angry pride and hid it behind a smile. "You remember my son, Culley, and my daughter, Maggie."

Webb Calder acknowledged the boy's presence with nod. The black-haired boy paled under the look and mumbled a stiff, "Morning, sir." Then Calder looked at the girl.

"Shouldn't you be in school, Maggie?" It was a question that held disapproval.

Actually, her name wasn't Maggie. It was Mary Frances Elizabeth O'Rourke, the same as that of her mother, who had died four years ago. But having two women in the family with the same name had been too confusing. Somewhere along the line, her father had started calling her Maggie, and it had stuck.

She shrugged a shoulder at the question. "My pa needed me today," she explained.

The truth was she missed more days of school than she attended. In the spring and fall, her father claimed he needed her to help on the ranch. Maggie had grown to realize that he was too lazy to work as long and as hard as he would have to by himself. The ranch was such a shoestring operation that they couldn't afford to hire help, so her father took advantage of her free labor.

During the winter, the tractor was broken down half the time, which meant they didn't have a snow blade to clear the five-mile drive to the road where she could catch the school bus. When her mother was alive, she'd saddled the horses and ridden with Culley and Maggie to the road on those occasions, then met them with the horses when the bus brought them back in the afternoon. But it was always too cold and too much trouble for her father.

Maggie no longer missed going to school. She had outgrown her clothes and had little to wear, except blue jeans and Culley's old shirts. At fifteen, nearly sixteen, she was very conscious of her appearance. She had tried altering some of her mother's clothes to fit her, but the results had been poor at best. None of her classmates had actually ridiculed the way she dressed, but Maggie had seen their looks of pity. With all her pride, that had been enough to prompt her into accepting the excuses her father found for her to stay home.

Her mother had been adamant that both of her children receive an education. It was something Maggie remembered vividly, because it was one of the few issues that the otherwise meek woman wouldn't be swayed from, not by her husband's anger or his winning charm. So Maggie kept her schoolbooks at home and studied on her own, determined not to fail her mother in this, as her father had failed her so often.

The disapproval that was in Webb Calder's look just reinforced her determination to keep studying. Maggie made no excuses for what her father was—a weak-willed man filled with empty promises and empty dreams. All the money in the world wouldn't make her father into the strong man Webb Calder was. It was a hard and bitter thing to recognize about your own father. And Maggie resented Webb Calder for presenting such a stark example of what her father could never be.

Realizing the conversation was going nowhere, Angus O'Rourke turned his gaze to the herd gathered in the hollow of the plains. His face took on the expression of one reluctant to leave good company but had work to be done.

"Well, I see a Shamrock brand or two in the herd." He collected the reins to back his horse before turning it toward the cattle. "I'll just cut out my few strays and head them back to their own side of the fence."

"I'll have one of my boys help you." Webb started to raise a hand to signal one of his men.

"We can manage," Maggie inserted. They may be poor, but she wasn't short on pride. She'd been taught by her mother never to accept favors unless she could return them someday, and it was ludicrous to think a Calder would ever need a favor from them.

Webb Calder's hand remained poised midway in the air while he looked silently at her father for confirmation that they wanted no help. "The three of us can handle it," her father stated to back up her claim, although he would have readily accepted the offer if she hadn't spoken up.

The hand came down to rest on the saddlehorn. "As you wish, Angus."

As he turned his horse, Angus flashed Maggie a black look and rode toward the herd. She and Culley trailed after him. Feeling the Triple C riders looking at them, Maggie sat straighter in the saddle, conscious of their overall shabby appearance, from their clothes to their ragged saddle blankets.

From the far side of the herd, Chase watched the motley trio of riders approach. Nate Moore had already passed the old man's orders around, so he knew one of the three riders was female. Buck let his horse sidle closer to Chase.

"How do you tell which one's the girl?" Buck's low voice was riddled with biting mockery.

"It must be the small one." Chase let a smile drift across his face. "She's supposed to be the youngest."

"She's young, all right," Buck agreed dryly. "I like my women with a little more age on 'em and more meat on their bones. Crenshaw was telling me this morning that Jake Loman has him a new blonde 'niece' working in his bar."

"That right?" Chase murmured, aware, as everyone was, that Jake's "nieces" were prostitutes. "That man does have a big family, doesn't he?"

Buck grinned. "When this roundup is over, you

and me are going to have to check her out. She might know some new tricks of the trade."

"Another week of looking at these cattle, and I'll be satisfied if all the new girl knows is the old tricks," Chase replied and turned his horse to head off an errant cow, succeeding in changing its mind about leaving the herd.

By then, Buck had returned to his former position several yards ahead of Chase. And there was no purpose in trying to resume that particular conversation. The O'Rourke family worked the herd to cut out their strays, while Chase and the other riders kept the cattle loosely bunched.

# Calder Born, Calder Bred

———◆━◆❮❯◆━◆———

# 1

THE WINDSWEPT MONTANA plains rolled with empty monotony beneath a freeze-dried sky. Along a fence line that stretched into the far-flung horizon, old snow formed low drifts. A brooming wind had brushed clean the brown carpet of frozen grass that covered the rough-and-tumble roll of the plains and held the thin layer of soil in place.

There was no room in this bleak, rough country for anyone not wise to its ways. To those who understood it, its wealth was given. But those who tried to take it eventually paid a brutal price.

Its primitive beauty lay in the starkness of its landscape. The vast reaches of nothingness seemed to go on forever. Winter came early and stayed late in this lonely land where cattle outnumbered people. The cattle on this particular million-acre stretch of empty range carried the brand of the Triple C, marking them as the property of the Calder Cattle Company.

A lone pickup truck was bouncing over the frozen ruts of the ranch road, just one of some two hundred miles of private roads that interlaced the Triple C Ranch. A vaporous cloud from the engine's exhaust trailed behind the pickup in a gray-white plume. Like the road, the truck seemed to be going nowhere. There was no destination in sight until the truck crested a low rise in the plains and came upon a hollow that nature had scooped into the deceptively flat-appearing terrain.

The camp known as South Branch was located in this large pocket of ground, one of a half-dozen such camps that formed an outlying circle around the nucleus of the ranch, breaking its vastness into manageable districts. The term "camp" was a holdover from the early days when line camps were established to offer crude shelters to cowboys working the range far from the ranch's home buildings.

There was a weathered solidness and permanence to the buildings at South Branch, structures built to last by caring hands. Stumpy Niles, who managed this district of the ranch, lived in the big log home with his wife and three children. A log bunkhouse, a long squatty building set into the hillside, was not far from the barn and calving sheds in the hollow.

The truck stopped by the ranch buildings. Chase Calder stepped from the driver's side and unhurriedly turned up the sheepskin collar of his coat against the keening wind. Like his father and his father's father, the reins of the Triple C Ranch were in his hands. His grip had to be firm enough to curb the unruly, sure enough to direct the operations, and steady enough to ride out the rough patches.

Authority had rested long on his shoulders, and he had learned to carry it well. This land that bore his family's name had left its mark on him, weathering his face to a leather tan, creasing his strong features with hard experience, and narrowing his brown eyes which had to see the potential trouble lurking beyond the far horizon. Chase was on the wrong side of thirty, pushing hard at forty, and all those years had been spent on Calder land. It was ingrained in his soul, the same way his wife, Maggie, was ingrained in his heart.

The slam of the pickup's passenger door sounded loudly. Chase's glance swung idly to the tall, lanky boy coming around the truck to join him, but there was nothing idle about the inspection behind that look. This sixteen-year-old was his son. Ty had been born a Calder, but he hadn't been raised one, something Chase regretted more than the trouble that had driven Maggie and himself apart nearly sixteen years ago.

Those had been long years, a time forever lost to them. Her father's death had aroused too much bitterness and hatred toward anyone carrying the Calder name. He hadn't tried to stop her when she left; and he had made no attempt to find out where she went. There had been no reason to try—or so he had thought at the time. But he hadn't known of the existence of his son until the fifteen-year-old boy had arrived, claiming him as his father. As much as he loved Maggie, at odd moments he resented that she had never told him about Ty. During their years of separation, Ty had grown to near manhood in a soft environment of southern California.

All this land would be Ty's someday, but precious years of training had been lost. Chase was nagged by the feeling that he had to cram fifteen years of experience into Ty in the shortest period of time possible. The kid had potential. He had try, but he was only greenbroke, like a young horse that wasn't sure about the rider on its back or the bit in its mouth—or what was expected from it.

With school out of session for spring break, Chase was taking advantage of the time to expose Ty to another facet of the ranch's operation—the ordeal of spring calving. For the regular cowboys, it was a seven-day-a-week job until the last cow had calved in all the districts of the Triple C Ranch. Since Stumpy Niles was shorthanded, Chase had brought Ty to help out and, at the same time, learn something more about the business.

As he stopped beside him, Ty hunched his shoulders against the bitter March wind rolling off the unbroken plains. In a comradely gesture, Chase threw a hand on his son's shoulder, heavily padded by the thick winter coat.

"You met most of the boys here when you worked the roundup last fall." Chase eyed his son with a hint of pride, not really noticing the strong family resemblance of dark hair and eyes and roughly planed features. It was the glint of determination he saw, and the slightly challenging thrust of Ty's chin.

Ty's memory of the roundup wasn't a pleasant one, so he just nodded at the information and held silent on his opinion of "the boys." They had made his life miserable. The worst horses on the ranch had been put in his string to ride. When "the boys" weren't throwing their hats under his horse, they were hoorahing him for grabbing leather when the horse started bucking or they were slapping his hands with a rope. If he forgot to recheck the saddle cinch before mounting, it was a sure bet one of them had loosened it. They had told him so many wild tales about the tricks to catch a steer that Ty felt if they had told him to shake salt on its tail, he would have been gullible enough to believe them.

They had pulled more practical jokes on him than he cared to remember. The worst had been waking up one morning and finding a rattlesnake coiled on top of his chest. It had been hibernating and the cold made it too sluggish to do anything, but Ty hadn't known that. He had damned near crapped his pants, and all "the boys" had stood around and laughed their sides out.

It was like being the new kid on the block. Of course, Ty never used that phrase around his father. His father had the opinion that city life made a man weak. More than anything else, Ty wanted to prove to his father that he wasn't weak, but he didn't know how much more of this endless hazing he could take. A couple of the old-timers, Nate Moore for one, had told him that all new men went through this, but it seemed to Ty that they were doing an extra job on him.

The hand on his shoulder tightened as his father

spoke again. "Stumpy's probably in the calving sheds. Let's go find him and get you settled in."

"Okay." Stirring, Ty reluctantly lifted his gaze to the sheds where there was a suggestion of activity.

A pigtailed girl about ten years old crawled between the railings of a board fence and ambled toward them. A heavy winter coat with patches and mismatched buttons gave bulk to her skinny frame, as did the double layer of jeans tucked inside a pair of run-down and patched boots. A wool scarf tied her cowboy hat on her head, a pair of honey-brown braids poking out the front.

"H'lo, Mr. Calder." She greeted Chase with the proper respect, but it was that of a youngster toward an elder rather than any degree of servility.

"Hello, Jess." A faint smile eased the tautness around his mouth as Chase recognized Stumpy's oldest child.

From the start, Jessy Niles had been a tomboy. Stumpy always claimed it was because, when she was teething, they'd let her chew on a strip of braided rawhide rein. She played with ropes and bridle bits when other girls were playing with dolls. She preferred tagging after her father to helping her mother in the kitchen or looking after her two brothers who followed her in succession.

There was never any little-girl cuteness about

her. She'd been like a gangly filly, all arms and legs, and skinny to boot. She wasn't homely, but her features were too strong—the cheekbones prominent and the jawline sharply angling. Her coloring was bland, her hair a washed-out brown, and her eyes an ordinary hazel—except they gleamed with intelligence, always direct, and sometimes piercing.

"I saw you drive up," she announced as she turned to size up Ty. "I told my dad you were here, so he'll probably be out shortly."

Ty bristled faintly under her penetrating stare. Even though he had become used to adults measuring him against his father, it was irritating to have this child slide him under her microscope. He gritted his teeth. He was sick of having to prove himself to everyone he met.

"You haven't met Stumpy's daughter, have you?" Chase realized and made the introductions. "This is Jessy Niles. My son, Ty."

She pushed a gloved hand at him, and Ty grudgingly shook it. "I heard about ya," she stated, and Ty bitterly wondered what that meant. It didn't sit well to think of some pigtailed kid laughing about some of the dumb things he'd done. "We've got a lot of first-calf heifers this year, so we sure could use the help." Jess spoke as if she were in charge. "Do you know anything about calving?"

A response seemed to be expected of him, from both his father and the young girl. Ty knew better than to claim knowledge he didn't possess. "No, but I've helped with a lot of foaling," he answered tersely.

The youngster wasn't impressed. "It's not quite the same. A mare's contractions are a lot more powerful than a cow's, so the birthing doesn't take as long." The information was absently tossed out, as if it were something everyone should know.

"How's it going?" inquired Chase.

"So far, we've only lost one calf," she said with a lift of her shoulders that seemed to indicate it was too soon to make a prognosis. Then a flash of humor brought a sparkle to her eyes. "Three of the boys already told Dad they were quitting at the end of the month and drawing their pay to head south. That's one ahead of this time last year."

Chase chuckled in his throat, fully aware more cowboys threatened to quit during calving season than any other time, although few actually did. His gaze lifted past the girl to watch Stumpy's approach from the calving sheds, his footsteps crunching on the frozen ground.

"Here comes my dad," Jessy said, turning her head.

Stumpy Niles was a squatly built man, needing

the nearly two-inch riding heels on his boots to reach the five-foot-seven-inch mark. But what he lacked in size he made up for in skill and stamina. He was always ready to laugh, but at the same time he was serious about his work and responsibility. Like Chase, Stumpy had been born and raised on the ranch; his grandfather had worked for Chase's grandfather, and the tradition was being carried on by succeeding generations. There were several families on the ranch that had never known any other home. No one retired when they grew old; they were simply given easier jobs.

At ten years, Jessy Niles already came to her father's shoulder. There was no resemblance to mark them as father and daughter. She was long-legged and skinny, while he was short and compact. His hair was dark, nearly black; so were his eyes. Energy seemed to be coiled inside him, always just below the surface, while she appeared quiet and contained.

After an exchange of greetings, Stumpy inserted, "We sure can use the help. They couldn't have picked a better time to let kids out of school for spring vacation."

"Nearly everyone's son on the Triple C is being put to work in the calving sheds," Chase remarked. "There's no reason for Ty to be an exception. You just tell him where you want him to go and what you want him to do."

Stumpy looked at Ty. "You might as well take your gear over to the bunkhouse and catch some rest if you can. We work the sheds in two shifts. You'll be on the night crew, so you'll be goin' on duty at five and workin' till six in the morning."

Figures, Ty thought, but he kept the rancor to himself. If there was a rotten job or lousy hours to be had, he always got them. His father had warned him it would be like this until he had proved himself, but Ty had never dreamed this testing would last so long. He was expected to endure the razzing and hazing without complaint, but the frustration was mounting inside him and the pressure from outside was only adding to the strain. More than anything else in this world, he wanted to make his father proud of him, but that day seemed farther away all the time.

"I'll take him to the bunkhouse for you, Dad," Jessy volunteered, "and show him where everything is."

"You do that." Her father smiled and nodded his approval.

"Where's your outfit?" Jessy turned to Ty and gave him another one of her level looks. Although it didn't show, she liked this strong-faced and lanky-muscled boy, even if he thought a rope honda was some kind of motorbike. That was a real shame, him being a Calder and all.

"In the back of the truck." The cold seemed to make him talk through his teeth, or so Jessy thought, not recognizing the irritation that hardened his jaw. "I'll get it."

After Ty had hauled his war bag and bulky bedroll out of the rear bed of the pickup, Jessy started for the chinked-log bunkhouse and glanced around to make sure he was following.

"I'll be back Sunday afternoon to pick you up, Ty," Chase called after his son and saw the bob of the cowboy hat in acknowledgment. He watched the pair walk silently toward the bunkhouse but directed his words to Stumpy. "A lot of people think ranchers leave cows to their own devices to drop their calves out on the range at the mercy of the elements, predators, and birthing complications."

It was an indirect way of saying that was what Ty had thought until Chase had explained differently. That's the way it had been done a hundred years ago, but certainly not now.

"That cow and her calf are too valuable to leave it all up to nature. Eight times out of ten, a cow won't have any trouble, but those two times, it pays to have a two-legged critter around to help out," Stumpy declared, then snorted out a laugh, his breath coming out in a billowing vapor cloud. "Hell, most city folks think all a rancher or a cowboy does is turn a cow loose with a bull, let her calve, and round 'em up in the spring to brand 'em and again in the fall to take them to market. They don't think about the castrating, dehorning, vaccinating, doctoring, and feeding—not to mention all the grief they give ya in between."

"Yeah, we got an easy life, Stumpy, and don't know it." His mouth was pulled into a wry line as he continued to watch the pair of youngsters approaching the bunkhouse. "That's quite a girl you've got there. She has her mother's looks, doesn't she?"

It wasn't really a question, since Chase had known Judy Niles almost as long as Stumpy had. She was a genial, sandy-haired woman, a couple inches taller than her husband, and attractive in an average sort of way.

"You should see her in those calving sheds, pulling calves in subzero temperatures." Stumpy puffed up a bit with pride. "The two boys, Ben and Mike, spend more time horsing around than helping. 'Course, they're young yet. But Jessy, she pitches right in there without being asked. As long as she wants to do it, I'm not going to stop her. It's a pity she isn't a boy. She's got the makings of a top hand."

"She'll outgrow this tomboy stage when she discovers boys." Chase winked in amusement.

"Probably," Stumpy agreed and showed a reluctance for that coming day. "I know her mother would like it if she helped more around the house. Speaking of mothers—" He paused, lifting his head to cast an interested look at Chase. "How's Maggie?"

"The doctor says she's doing fine. Nothing to worry about." A glowing warmth seemed to radiate from the brown depths of his eyes, an inner pride bursting forth.

"It's getting close to her time, isn't it?" Stumpy asked, frowning slightly as he tried to recall.

"The first of May, so she's got a little over two months before the baby is due." But he wasn't as calm or casual about the coming event as he tried to appear. "The senator is flying in with some people he wants me to meet, so I'd better be getting back to The Homestead."

As Ty followed the girl across the threshold into the bunkhouse, he heard the truck starting up and looked over his shoulder to see the pickup reverse to turn onto the single road leading away from the camp. He knew he was completely on his own again. A wary tension strung his senses to a high pitch of alertness as he swung the door shut and turned to face the room.

He was standing in a small common room. A table and a collection of chairs stood in one corner, and a sofa and a couple of armchairs, all showing the scars of cowboys' indifference, occupied the other corner. A converted barrel heater split the room in the middle, its sides glowing almost a cherry-red as it waged a continual combat to keep the cold outside temperatures from invading the bunkhouse. Propped against the back wall, there was a broken chair to to used for kindling in the wood stove. A variety of cartoons, western pictures, and pinup girls were tacked to the walls in a crazy quilt of decoration.

"The bathroom's through that door." Jessy pointed to the right and walked to the barrel heater to warm her hands. "The beds are in there." She indicated the opposite direction with a nod of her hatted head. "You can take your pick of the empty ones."

Ty hefted his duffel bag a little higher to change his grip on it and headed for the open doorway on his left. The sleeping area of the bunkhouse was thinly partitioned into small rooms, furnished with plain wire-and-steel frame beds with a cowboy's bedroll serving as mattress and blanket. The first few beds, the ones closest to the common room and able to benefit from the wood stove's heat, were all occupied, either by possessions or by quilted shapes actually sleeping in the beds. Ty stopped at the first empty bunk he found and tossed his duffel bag and thick bedroll onto the wire frame. Coat hooks were screwed into the wall to hold his hat and coat and the odd piece of clothing or two.

"Did ya find one?" The girl's querying voice searched him out.

"Yeah." He half turned away from the doorway and began shrugging out of his heavy jacket. His thermal underwear and wool shirt were more than adequate in the relative warmth of the bunkhouse.

Her footsteps stopped at the doorway. "If you don't feel like layin' down right away, there's coffee in the pot on the hot plate."

"No, thanks." Ty left his hat on but hung up his coat and turned to untie his bedroll and spread it open on the bed.

He caught her out of the corner of his eye, leaning against the doorway, her coat unbuttoned and the scarf loose around her neck. He wished she'd quit watching him with those measuring eyes. It made him uncomfortable. He noticed the cup of steaming coffee in her now-ungloved hand. She lifted it to her wide mouth, blowing to cool it even as she sipped at the hot, thickly black coffee. He still couldn't stomach the strong coffee everyone on the ranch drank with such regularity unless he drowned it in milk.

"You shouldn't be drinking that stuff." He jerked the string tying his bedroll and unrolled the mattresslike quilt pad with its sheets, quilt, and canvas tarp bound inside. "It'll stunt your growth."

"I been drinking coffee since I was six." Scoffing amusement riddled her voice. "I'd hate to think how tall I'd be now if I hadn't." She paused, then added for good measure, "And it hasn't made my hair curly or grown hair on my chest."

After he had the pad and blankets straightened out, Ty set the duffel bag with his clothes and shaving kit at the head of the bed for a pillow. When the girl showed no signs of leaving, he stretched himself out the full length of the bed and set his hat forward on the front of his face.

"I'm going to get some rest," Ty said, in case she hadn't got the message. The hat partially muffled his voice.

"See you tonight," Jessy Niles replied, not finding his behavior in the least rude, and straightened from the doorway to saunter down the hall to the common room.

As the sound of her footsteps retreated, Ty pushed his hat back. Raising his arms, he cupped the back of his head in his hands and stared at the ceiling. There was a rawness in him that was close to pain. He had no one to turn to, no one to whom he could talk out his frustrations. He was too old to go crying to his mother, and since it was his father's respect he so desperately wanted to earn, he couldn't very well go running to him with his troubles. He wanted to work them out on his own, but so far no one was giving him a chance. There were so many things to learn that just when he felt he was grasping the rudiments of one thing, something new was thrown at him, and always the hazing and the handing out of misinformation until he felt like some gullible dimwit.

The return trip to The Homestead, the name given to the house occupied by the head of the Triple C, took the best part of two hours. The sleek twin-engine plane parked by the private airstrip near the buildings of the ranch's headquarters advised Chase that Senator Bulfert had arrived in his absence.

Leaving the truck parked in front of the imposing two-story house, Chase mounted the steps to the wide porch running the length of the south front and crossed to the solid wood double doors. The house had been built decades ago with a craftsman's care and possessed that rare quality of character. Two hundred years from now it would still be standing and, if Chase had his way, a Calder would still be living in it.

When he entered the large open foyer, Chase heard voices coming from the study on his left. Doug Trumbo, one of the ranch hands, was carrying an armload of luggage up the staircase leading from the living room to the second floor and its guest bedrooms.

With a shift in direction, Chase headed for the open doors of the den, where his guests had obviously gathered. Upon entering, his glance first sought out Maggie. She was sitting in a chair near the window, her black hair gleaming in the sunlight and an arm resting on the protruding roundness of her stomach. The sight of her always had the power to stir a hungry response in him while at the same time evoking feelings that were profoundly tender.

Her smile greeted him as Chase walked to her chair, pulling off his gloves and stuffing them in his coat pocket. Even as his attention was divided by the guests in the room, he was reaching to take her small hand in his large one.

"I'm sorry I wasn't on hand when you arrived," Chase apologized and let his gaze travel over his four guests. The ruddy-faced senator and his aide, Wes Govern, he already knew.

"No problem. Made better time than we thought. Had a good tail wind," the quick-talking senator replied. Age was beginning to sag his round cheeks, leaving jowls and pockets under his eyes. "Just arrived a few minutes ago. Wes hasn't had time to pour a round of drinks yet." With a slight turn of his head, he issued a booming directive to his assistant. "Chase drinks whiskey, Wes."

"I remember." The man nodded and added another glass to the liquor tray.

"How have things been? Well, I hope," the senator declared and continued without giving Chase an opportunity to respond. "No more land purchases you need my help with, are there?" he inquired with a conspiratorial wink.

"None." There was a dryness about Chase's eyes at the reference to the purchase of ten thousand acres of land from the government that Bulfert had arranged some years ago. It was the last parcel of previously leased land to come under the Calder title. He now owned all the land that constituted the Triple C Ranch.

"Chase, I want you to meet Eddy Joe Dyson."

The politician curved an arm around the shoulders of a slightly built man, the gesture and body language suggesting to Chase that the two were united in their cause, whatever it was. "Been looking forward to getting the two of you together for quite a while. E. J., meet Chase Calder."

Chase stepped away from Maggie's side to shake hands with the older man, dressed in an expensive navy pinstripe suit, styled in western lines with a yoked front and boot-cut pants. Chase put the man's age somewhere in the middle forties. The man's hand was smooth of any calluses, and his skin didn't have the leathery tan of a cattleman despite the white felt Stetson on his head.

"Welcome to the Triple C, Mr. Dyson." The western clothes were just a facade, but Chase didn't detect any shallowness in the level gaze that returned his silent inspection. If anything, he noted a hint of shrewdness.

"It's my pleasure," the man drawled. "And my friends call me E. J. I'd be pleased if you and your wife did the same." He half turned to invite the second man forward. "This is my business partner, George Stricklin."

Ten years younger, tall, with yellow hair, the man wore gold wire glasses which he removed and slipped precisely into the breast pocket of his suit jacket. Despite his athletic build, there was a studious and silent quality about him. His fingers were long and finely shaped, and Stricklin did no more than nod when he shook hands with Chase.

Dyson spoke again. Angling his head toward Maggie, he inclined it in a courtly gesture. "I must say that I thought our Texas ladies couldn't be matched for beauty, but I've been forced to revise my opinion since meeting your lovely wife."

"I believe I'm much more prejudiced," Chase murmured and glanced backward into Maggie's vibrantly green eyes. Now that the phase of morning sickness had passed, she looked positively radiant. He'd heard it said that women were more beautiful when they were pregnant and had dismissed it. But he was now willing to concede that it might be in the eye of the beholder, because Maggie had never looked more beautiful to him than she did this minute.

"You're from Texas?" Maggie inserted, skillfully directing the conversation away from flattering comments about her. No matter how healthy and happy she felt, there was still that feeling of gaucheness and awkwardness which insisted compliments be turned aside.

"Yes." The slow, twanging drawl in his voice was both smooth and attractive, like oiled leather.

"That set of horns above the mantel makes me feel right at home, too," he said, indicating the mounted pair of longhorns on the massive stone fireplace that dominated the room with its size and cheery log fire.

"They belonged to a Texas steer. I guess you could say this ranch was founded on Texas longhorns," Chase admitted and accepted the short glass of whiskey and ice from the senator's aide.

"I remember your father telling me your family came from the Fort Worth area." The senator took a fat cigar from his pocket, then glanced inquiringly at Maggie, who silently nodded her permission. "That's E. J.'s home turf." He felt his pockets for a light, but his assistant produced a lighter before the senator found one. "Something of an entrepreneur, eh, E. J.?"

The relationship between Dyson and his partner had always struck the senator as an unusual one. Once he had described Stricklin as the brains of the company and Dyson as the guts of it. Every act, every move, of the silent Stricklin was deliberately thought out beforehand by that computer-like mind. Logic and reason dictated his decisions. But Dyson acted on instinct and had the guts to gamble on his hunches. It was a curious blend in a partnership, one balancing the other, with Dyson naturally appearing to be the dominant member of the team.

"I do have several business interests," Dyson admitted while eyeing Chase as if he were the source of his next.

"If you're thinking of venturing into the cattle-ranching business, it means investing a lot of money in nondepreciable assets," Chase warned dryly.

There was a quick glance exchanged between the politician and the Texan. "I guess you could say I'm more interested in what's under the ground than what's on top of it. Which is why I asked the senator to introduce me to you. I dabble in oil and natural-gas exploration."

An eyebrow quirked in mild curiosity as Chase let the statement sink in. Taking his time, he set his glass down on the table by Maggie's chair and shed his coat. The flames crackled in the fireplace, filling the brief silence.

"I think you're in the wrong part of Montana," Chase stated finally. "You want to be over in the Badlands, or in the Powder River country."

"Drilling companies are already working those fields," E. J. disagreed. "Now, I don't pretend to be an expert, but I try to hire them. I like to gamble my money on finding new fields, not striking it in old ones and having to fight the big companies."

"Am I to surmise that you're here because you think there is oil to be found on the Triple C?" Chase was vaguely bemused by the idea.

"If you know about the Powder River and the Badlands, then you must know they've made some finds near the base of the Rockies. They're near the western edge of your boundaries," he reminded Chase in a calm and knowing tone. "I could have brought my geologist with me and let him tell you all about rock strata—and how promising a section of your land looks. It wouldn't mean any more to you than it does to me, and I don't know one from the other. Now, Stricklin, he's gone over all the figures and calculations and says there is more than a good chance of finding oil. So I'm here to see about acquiring those rights."

There was no change in expression to indicate Chase's inner feelings. He looked at Maggie and took a sip of his drink. When his gaze finally returned to the man, it was sharply measuring.

"The subject is certainly open to discussion." He'd hear the man out, but it wasn't a decision he was going to make quickly.